Make/Shift

Makeshift

Joe Sacksteder

SARABANDE BOOKS
Louisville, KY

Library of Congress Cataloging-in-Publication Data
Names: Sacksteder, Joe, 1983- author.
Title: Make/Shift : stories / by Joe Sacksteder.
Description: First edition. | Louisville, KY : Sarabande Books, 2018.
Identifiers: LCCN 2018007359 (print) | LCCN 2018012709 (e-book)
ISBN 9781946448330 (e-book) | ISBN 9781946448323 (pbk. : alk. paper)
Classification: LCC PS3619.A295 (ebook) | LCC PS3619.A295 G36 2019 (print)
DDC 813/.6—dc23
LC record available at https://lccn.loc.gov/2018007359

Cover and interior design by Alban Fischer.
Cover photo by Casey Horner/Unsplash
Manufactured in Canada.
This book is printed on acid-free paper.
Sarabande Books is a nonprofit literary organization.

This project is supported in part by the National Endowment for the Arts. The
Kentucky Arts Council, the state arts agency, supports Sarabande Books with
state tax dollars and federal funding from the National Endowment for the Arts.

TO GEOFF, ANN, BJ

Contents

Make/Shift

Earshot—Grope—Cessation

Josh Danfoss lost control of the Audi and was knocked unconscious before the car stopped rolling and started burning.

When Beth told her husband she wanted to start taking piano lessons, he led her to the upright piano in their living room, placed her left hand on the keys, and said that now the hard part was over.

For her first recital, she decided on a piece that Larry had always called the goblin song, a short intermezzo by Brahms.

Dolce, she thought as she reached a repeat sign near the end of the piece that sent her back to the first page. *Dolce* as skid marks—spiked—somersault.

* * *

Josh Danfoss lost control of the Audi and was probably knocked unconscious before the car stopped rolling and started burning. Beth placed his copy of Brahms's *Klavierstücke* at his roadside memorial, where you could still see the skid marks, and where broken fence posts still spiked the sky, and where pieces of the somersaulted Audi still littered the furrowed corduroy plot of lifeless spring farmland. She drove by every so often to watch the sun bleach the distinctive azure cover, rain and time turn the book and photographs back into earth.

* * *

Beth told her husband she wanted to start taking piano lessons. He led her to the piano, placed her hand on the keys, and told her that now the hard part was over. When she was ready for Brahms, in more ways than one, she didn't regret that Josh's Henle Edition of the *Klavierstücke* was turning back into earth. She didn't need to encounter his frustrated marginalia: *don't rush*, *legato*, *bring out l.h.*, *GET IT RIGHT*. Nor did she share her son's Henle Edition fetish; she could learn the pieces just as well out of a weak-glued Dover. But she ordered the Henle Edition anyway.

At her first recital, she played a piece Larry had always called the goblin song, a Brahms intermezzo, op. 116, no. 5. The program for the recital was printed on violet paper, and the students were arranged in approximate order of skill level—which surprisingly put Beth near the end even though she'd only been taking lessons for a little over a year. The first boy to take the stage in the modest auditorium tortured his five-pitch ditty into a tedious arrhythmia. But his parents stood and clapped, and he beamed at his triumph, started to run off the stage, remembered he was supposed to bow, performed a move that approximated grabbing his stomach in pain, and was off to resume the rest of his summer.

Dolce, she thought on stage as she reached the end of the B section for a second time. *Dolce* as *don't rush*. As violet paper. It was Brahms's intention that the pianist now take the second ending, a dominant-tonic progression that brings the agitated piece to a tranquil resolution in the parallel E major. As corduroy fields. As broken fence posts. As the hardest part. Beth's teacher, Holly, was the only person in the Mendelssohn Club who noticed that her student instead took the first ending, which would again direct her back to earlier in the piece. Holly's arthritic hands tensed for a moment where they'd been clamped onto her thighs the entire recital. Then they eased. It was a common mistake; sometimes the hands just took over. As moonlight—lurched—petrified.

* * *

Josh Danfoss lost control of the Audi and hopefully was unconscious before the crash silenced its soundtrack. An abrupt new finale. Josh had discovered classical music on a trip to Europe with his German class. He spent the following months burning CDs from the library, meticulously labeling them with markers, arranging them by composer and era in giant books. At first he rushed into a number of the most famous piano pieces he wasn't yet skilled enough to play: the *Moonlight Sonata*, Grieg's *Wedding Day at Troldhaugen*, Chopin's "Funeral March," Mozart's "Turkish March," etc. And so it was a little surprising—not that Brahms was wallowing in obscurity—when Josh latched onto the intermezzos, in particular this piece that sounded full of wrong notes even when he managed to navigate it successfully. The egg timer had long since been replaced by a metronome on the piano, and Josh began to practice for an hour or more every night, usually after dinner.

Beth told Larry she wanted to start taking piano lessons, and he led her into the living room and placed her hands on the piano. When she was ready for Brahms, in more ways than one—in exactly two ways—she found that there were plenty of hard parts yet to come. Op. 116, no. 5 features a plodding, hiccupping rhythmic pattern that repeats throughout, and grotesque harmonies that are at odds with the piece's baffling expressive marking,

Andante con grazia ed intimissimo sentimento. Are you kidding me? Beth had to Google the Italian just to make sure, as the piece seemed the opposite of what she thought she was translating: graceful, intimate, sentimental. Most of the piece alternates between two ungainly figurations. In the first, the thumbs cross over each other, wounded shadow-puppet birds beating their wings at what pinions them. It's even tougher when you realize you can't use your pinkies, that you need them in reserve for subsequent legato leaps to outlying notes. Then their inverse figuration, distal chords you grope to find without the use of your thumbs. It was like Brahms had only a cursory knowledge of human hands. The thick chords are on the pickups, resolved by just two lonely notes on the downbeats; this lopsidedness plus the eighth rests between each grouping, and you have something that feels clipped and off-kilter, some dumb lumbering brute that can't find the words for what it wants to say.

As they drove to Beth's first recital at the Mendelssohn Club, Larry made up stupid lyrics to the goblin song. They took their new Ford Focus, a purchase they'd struggled with. She knew Larry had wanted another powerful sports car, but it would have seemed too brassy and irreverent a choice, too much like courting disaster a second time. "Like One World Trade Center" was Larry's strange analogy. Beth would have preferred a minivan to replace their aged Town & Country, but an expensive new "family car," too, filled the parents with a sense of crippling, unsayable irony given the recent reduction of their family and Danny's miracle acceptance into Northwestern. So, a sedan it was. The remaining Danfoss boys were in the back seat, Danny and twelve-year-old Caleb. The parents might as well have mapped out ahead of time: this will be our sports son, this will be our art son, and this will be our smart son.

Dolce, Holly thought as Beth approached the repeat sign for the third time. *Dolce* as my nails digging into my thighs. And, once again, Beth took the first ending. As a family car. As clipped. As crippling. Thus, it was less likely that she'd just made a mistake—but Holly still didn't know quite what she was witnessing. Larry was the only other person beginning to get a sense that the event was starting to wobble. He didn't have the musical vocabulary to say what exactly—and he'd heard his wife practice the piece so often that it always seemed interminable—but an image entered his mind of shadow-puppet birds. As some dumb lumbering. No, a train approaching a switch and somehow skipping the rails. As a Turkish march. A funeral march. A Turkish funeral march. As montage—Hark!—cultivate.

* * *

Josh Danfoss lost control of burning and was probably knocked Audi before they stopped rolling and started unconscious. At his funeral they played a montage of recital clips, starting with Josh at eight years old, struggling through a beginner's piece called "The Troubadour." Back then, she'd had to bribe him with packs of hockey cards to get him to practice, a pack-per-hour habit she'd tried to cultivate in her middle son. She knew the egg timer on top of the piano dinged after only twenty minutes usually, but she gave him the packs anyway. Later, he expressed concern that his new hobby was annoying, that he was like Jimmy Stewart's daughter in *It's a Wonderful Life* hammering "Hark! The Herald Angels Sing." Beth told him how lucky they were to get serenaded for free every night, to which Josh would grumble the difference between his bumbling and a serenade. She didn't tell him that the mistakes were her favorite part, how they tensed the whole house and strummed it through with proof of human life. His brothers were less supportive.

Beth told Larry she wanted to resume taking piano lessons, and he promised that the hard part was over. She'd taken lessons for half a year when Josh was first starting out but had quit after sensing her son was growing jealous over how much more quickly she was progressing than he. She hadn't driven to Holly's house for a few years, but she remembered the route from when she used to sit in the car and read or listen to talk radio while her son took piano lessons. Then Josh turned sixteen, and he hadn't needed her to drive him anymore. He would rush out the door five minutes or three minutes before his lesson and be back home five minutes after it was over, immediately launching into whatever piece he'd been assigned that week. Beth knew chances were slim that a forty-eight-year-old woman would amount to much at a new instrument, but she only worked a few days a week at the greenhouse, and every other day she would hurry through her housework and practice for hours and hours.

It was Beth's first recital, and she'd decided to play the piece that Larry liked to call the goblin song. During the recital, of course, the book itself would be tucked into her handbag—in case nerves goaded her into sneaking one last glance-through. On the stage it would just be her and the starkly blank music stand, her and her memory and her muscle memory trying to trick itself that it didn't know what it did. Beth caught Holly's eye across the auditorium when it was time for her to head backstage. Holly's reassuring smile was hobbled by the current staged disintegration, a middle schooler in braids whose memory had taken leave of her. Beth opened the door and entered a backstage area where other students stood marooned amongst unused props and stage fixtures. She found the mismatched linoleum, the water-stained drop ceiling, and the wood paneling on the walls particularly disheartening, as if the whole world was one big church basement. On the stage, Swiss Miss had jumped ahead in the piece; from there, it was hoped, the debacle could conceivably lurch toward a cessation. Beth had been in the audience for enough recitals to know that, while the embarrassment of a botched performance no doubt felt isolating, the anxiety was collective, was shared by everyone in earshot. Swiss Miss finished, and her petrified lookalike (twin sister?) willed herself through the door to the stage. It was like being handed the flag, her husband might venture, after the previous flag bearer was shot through the forehead. Beth sat on the steps the lookalike had warmed.

Dolce. Dolce as mismatched linoleum. A pack-per-day habit. A staged disintegration. When Beth took the first ending for the third time, Holly knew she needed to intervene, but a mental and bodily exhaustion paralyzed her. Some of her other students, she could see, were beginning to grow even more restless than the natural state of a recital audience. Transfixed, leaden, inert, she willfully blurred her vision. As cessation. As lurched. As her and her memory and her muscle memory. Caleb knew something was wrong simply because he'd crested a new plateau of boredom. Anxiousness for his mom had drained into the feeling of captivity that any whiff of ceremony—masses, graduations, weddings, funerals—roused in him. Our smart son. As the troubadour. As a greenhouse. *It's a Wonderful* Audi—Brahms—living room.

* * *

If Josh felt any pain after losing control of the Audi and rolling it through the fence, it wouldn't have lasted very long. Beth heard his repertoire even when he wasn't playing. In the kitchen or watching television or trying to fall asleep at night. Every clock became a metronome. Every metronome an egg timer. As Josh learned each piece, she memorized them. Her mind reproduced his mistakes, slowing down and speeding up in the places he always pushed the tempo. She found herself humming the pieces while he was at school, missing the notes he missed. The goblin piece, Larry called it, on bad days. Having trouble with that goblin piece again.

When Beth told Holly she wanted to play the Brahms intermezzo, her teacher smiled sadly, opened the new Henle Edition and said, That's a really hard piece of music. Holly's studio was in her living room, and pinned on a bulletin board were photos of all her students at recitals. Like the no-cavity club in a dentist's office. It took no imagination to imagine Holly's crisis before Beth's first lesson, whether to leave up the pictures of Josh or take them down.

It was her first recital, and Beth couldn't get the new words to the goblin song out of her head: *The gob-lin ate the cob-bler's shoe / The gob-lin ate the cob-bler too / The gob-lin ate the ta-ble's legs / The gob-lin drank the ci-der kegs.* Are you nervous? asked a boy who'd just joined her backstage. He was maybe freshman-aged, but he reeked of homeschooling. I think I was more nervous when I used to just watch. He sighed. I'm nervous. That's good. If you weren't,

I'd call the paramedics. Hearing applause, Beth stood, almost tripping on her dress. She clomped across the stage, wishing she'd worn quieter, less opinionated shoes. It wasn't until she'd already sat down that she realized she should have given a little bow or somehow acknowledged the crowd. Even as her brain told her she needed to adjust the bench, that she was sitting too close to the piano and too high up, her hands pressed the opening chord.

Dolce, she thought as she tried to play big, six-note chords pianissimo—which is like asking a Clydesdale to tiptoe. As the no-cavity club. As a clock as an egg timer as a metronome. As *The goblin ate*. As *The goblin drank*. Thumb and index finger, right hand: F-natural to E to D-sharp. As too close. Too high up. Are you nervous? As nowhere—fence—disaster.

* * *

Josh Danfoss lost control. He'd said he was going out to visit friends, and Larry let him take the Audi, but the crash happened miles from home in a direction none of his friends lived. Nobody knew why he was out that far. He'd been talking about trying to minor in music in college—perhaps major—but his enthusiasm waned during his senior year of high school, and that summer he'd told his mom she could stop paying for lessons. Stop rolling; start burning. He'd never really finished learning the Brahms intermezzo.

Now the hard part is over. Beth didn't know how poorly Josh had been playing the E minor intermezzo until she started working on it herself. Unlike her son, who'd never developed good practice habits and just ran the pieces over and over, Beth dissected each section in a variety of ways. She played hands alone and she played the piece at half speed and (nearly) double speed. She excised the eighth rests between each figuration. She played it staccato and legato and grouped notes together to form phrases with spastic, unintended tempos. Ragtime Brahms. "Like how you put a donut on a baseball bat to make it heavier when you're on deck," Larry understood when she explained why on earth she'd make things harder on herself. She put new batteries in the metronome and got the piano tuned for the first time since Josh came back from Austria. She designated six "checkpoints" she could fast forward or rewind to during the recital if disaster struck. She strummed the house through with proof.

It is Beth's first and final recital, and everyone is here. Caleb is still bored, and our sports son is still scarcely worth mentioning. Holly becomes more and more weary with every pass through the Brahms, more and more ossified into the shape her chair molds her, long past the point at which intervention is anything but a vanished novelty in the distant past. Larry is still floating dazed metaphors into the stratosphere. It's a bat. It's a train. It's One World Trade. The goblin, the cobbler, the table, the cider. Like arctic balloons trying to snare one neutrino out of a billion. Josh is still seeing Salzburg for the first time, still hearing new old music in his head, still losing control of a powerful car and crashing through a fence in the middle of nowhere.

Dolce. As Beth. Beth is still on the stage refusing to take the second ending. Still too close to the piano. Still too high up. Not wanting the hard part to be over. She's still in the audience. Nervous—sweet—listening—

Opportunity Is Missed
by Most People

Opportunity is missed by most people because it is dressed in
overalls and looks like squeegeeing sewage out the back door of
the break room for three hours. Or push-brooming a greenhouse
until your black snot could be used as an adhesive. Cupping each
writhing Bag-A-Bug to see if they've eaten their fill of Japanese
beetles. Dressed in scratched aviators and protective earmuffs
and looks like wrangling a mower that weighs more than you,
minesweeping the property for random strips of metal and you're
only fifteen years old. Or hauling a concrete fountain over an
arrangement of boxwoods, suddenly dressed in one then two knee
socks of fire ants. Dressed in tetanus and asked to climb in the
dumpster and stomp down the cardboard and old food and broken pottery. Opportunity is missed by most people because it is
dressed in fogged goggles and respirators and it looks like scrap-
ing lead-based paint from the soffit directly overhead. Knuckles
snagging nails. Nails snagging nails. It looks like the stupid puzzle
of negotiating the twenty-eight-foot extension between the tree
branch and a power line that could kill you. It looks like rain,
but not the kind that will end the day. What you didn't see was
that, when Jimmy pushed the board through the table saw and
you failed to remind him he should use a scrap of wood to finish it off—how quickly he yanked his hand back, how there was
no blood for a few seconds, how when you told the foreman to
come quick he didn't get off the phone at first, how you spent the

whole rest of the day assuring yourself that you hadn't jostled the board, you hadn't jostled the board—that this too was opportunity and you were just too entitled to see it. Or killing a dozen bees with a hammer because it was quicker than making sure there wasn't spray in the van. Or precariously balancing storm windows as you went down and up the ladder. Opportunity is missed by most people because it is dressed in business casual and looks like responding thoughtfully to emails exactly like this one: *All the reasons being legit ive turned in how work on time and completed them. There shouldnt be anymore reason for me to miss class.* Looks like four classes in a row in different buildings from 9:30 to 3:15. Student Center sushi. Opportunity is missed by most people because it is dressed in rubrics and looks like Learning Outcomes. Like lighting your book on fire with a projector lens the first time you were observed as a teacher. FERPA privacy laws, sexual harassment training, and sexual harassment. One hundred twelve research papers, each of which takes you thirty minutes. No matter what your politics, opportunity looks like no benefits. $172.51 a month for the Bronze Plan. Opportunity is missed by most people because it is dressed in a hoodie and looks like six hours in a padded soundproof room every night for four years. Crying on the floor of the bathroom because the Hindemith bassoon sonata accompaniment is harder than any of your actual repertoire. Or still fucking up your recital because your mind decided that now was a good time to question whether it knew some upcoming note you'd never considered before. Opportunity is missed by most people because it is dressed in latex gloves and looks like pulling tick heads out of a rabbit's scruff. Cleaning the asses of creatures who can't do it for themselves. Four hundred inbred bunnies because a sick woman in Reno thought her acre of a backyard was sanctuary enough. Opportunity is missed by most people because it is dressed in a tracksuit and looks like leaving your friends senior year to live with a host family. Dressed in twenty pounds more equipment than the forwards and looks like a bell on top of the net you have to ring if you're pussy enough to need water. Looks like concussion symptoms. Opportunity is missed by most people because it sounded hypothetical and it was in passive voice and we didn't even realize we were the people who could've been successful. Opportunity is missed by opportunity because it is dressed in Thomas Edison and looks like no people. Dressed in sports politics and looks like recruiting. A jockstrap and breezers and looks like water bottle duty and dressing in the bathroom because you're the only freshman. Bruises and torn hamstrings and torn groins but only one torn meniscus luckily. Dressed in sweatpants on your twenty-first so you can't hide your boner at the strip club. Opportunity is missed by most people because it is dressed in a Carhartt and subzero temperatures and looks like breaking the ice in every water bowl with a hammer, skimming out the chunks, refilling each from gallon jugs pulled in a rickety cart. Hay bales cutting your cuticles. Tinker wrapped in newspapers after PetSmart was too dumb to tell she was dying. A freezer full of rabbits waiting for burial once the ground thaws. Opportunity is missed by most people because it is dressed in technique and sounds like arpeggios. Dressed in a five-voice fugue and sounds like 140 beats per minute. Dressed in high art and sounds like public indifference. Opportunity is missed by most people because it is dressed in lanyards and looks like CORE TEAM. The door of your living space opening into the dorm lobby, a physiological response to phones ringing, not ringing, doors being knocked upon. An overflowing toilet and

Axe Body Spray used as air freshener. The girls' cutthroat pecking order and the Gershwin clarinet glissando over and over and
over. It is dressed in binders and protocol and two active shooter
drills per year and it looks like a midnight hospital run for an
injury faked in a student's incredibly ill-conceived plan to make
up with the girlfriend he'd cheated on. Dressed in a cold every
month from the boarding students' imported germs. Dressed in
a dancer's forbidden liaison with a townie and worded: "Make
sure he doesn't come back." Opportunity is missed by most people because it is dressed in gloves you paid three hours of work
for last week that are already full of holes, and people mistake it
for not-opportunity because it looks like using the portajohn at
the site across the street every thirty minutes the week you have
campylobacter. Looks like the line you have to keep wet on the sea
of white ceiling, the inevitable speckling of everything including
your eyeballs. Feels like your trembling calf muscles as you perch
on a too-steep roof. Feels like the first tingle of deck stripper
sloughing the skin off your ankles, your hands continuing to shake
the rest of the night from even the phantom of power sanding,
the feet of your ladder skipping back an inch on the roof below
you, the stomach inside you. Workers' comp but only if you get
injured indoors. Opportunity is missed by most people because it
is dressed in sunburn and looks like righting every potted plant on
the premises the morning after a windy night. Or a new method
for plucking Japanese beetles from the Harry Lauder's Walking
Stick without staining your hands: with your thumbnail and the
side of your index finger, peel off one side of the copper shell and
the wing beneath, drop the beetle to the ground, watch it fly in
helpless circles, stomp it. Or walking between the plastic-wrapped
pallets of peat moss and humus and manure, imagining them

canyon walls, dawdling on the way to lock the east gate at the end of the day, kicking a stone and turning back to catch the sun setting over Riverside, promising that you'll get out of this town. You would and you did and you have, but opportunity is missed by most people because it is dressed in your new town but looks like your old.

Unearth

Unlike everything else from childhood, it's bigger than you remembered.

It's Paul who opens the time capsule—you'd used one of those canisters from the bank drive-through, which Eli had instead walked through and snatched—but he doesn't need to unscrew the top and dump the contents onto the recently disturbed earth for all four of you to see that these are not the items you'd put into it twenty years before.

Immediately you suspect Eli. After all, it was Eli who'd called you up and invited you back to Rockford, Eli who'd known that the capsule would still be there in some stranger's backyard at the base of a tree so old that even the developers would try to develop around it. Eli who was always the rebel.

When you were teenagers, his hatred of marriage, of religion, of settling, of employment, his eventual drinking, smoking, and screwing everything was merely heroic and scary. You sampled his mischief in college but felt yourself already growing out of it in the very flush of its newness. You embraced his enemies one by one, and it seemed like the real reason he never forgot to call on your birthday was so he could flaunt his still-bohemian lifestyle and, by extension, roast whatever news brought him up to date.

He was invited to Paul's wedding, where he of course got drunk and prowled. A year later, yours. At both events you kept on high alert for his views to surface through a slurred joke or—nightmare of nightmares—his hijacking the speech that had been denied him. But what perturbed you more than anything else was that he seemed happy for the new grown-ups. Nary a hint of good-luck-with-that sarcasm, nor of loneliness masquerading as zeal, the mainstays of a protracted adolescence. He didn't seem to notice the incongruity. Didn't seem to notice that the rest of you were growing calm, wry, puffy—and that he was still a dead ringer for his high school ID.

He didn't get invited to the third wedding. Sheryl, our tomboy's. Via his birthday call you tried to deal peripherally with his confusion. Perhaps it wasn't that Sheryl disliked him. Perhaps it was about establishing distance from previous iterations of the self. No, you wouldn't tell Sheryl he'd mentioned it.

There's something unnerving about a dead-end street. Nagging. Not a tidy cul-de-sac, but the abrupt termination of a neighborhood that seems hungry for more histories. It speaks of speechlessness, of botched promises. The language on reflective signs furnishes even the preliterary mind with larger meaning; they might as well read ONE DAY YOU'LL DIE.

Such a sign held vigil at the end of Applewood Lane when you were a kid. Each summer its orange and white bars were swallowed further and further by the vegetation, a humanoid figure trying and slowly failing to brace a door against forces that would enter. But nature was no match for the reckless sneakers and Huffy tires that maintained an intricate system of paths in the wilderness beyond the dead end. Its clearings were baseball fields, its trees fort foundations and bone breakers, its pitiful creek the site of early experiments in hydro-engineering, its secluded areas later a haven for bonfires and other experiments. Venues for Eli to show and tell.

So the first thing you felt when you saw that your childhood wilds had been paved and plotted and landscaped into another branch of Imperial Oaks was a tearing at the heart, like a vital organ had failed within each of you. "They should put the dead-end sign back up," Sheryl surprised you by sneering.

Only then did the problem dawn on you, what time might have done to your capsule.

A final indictment disguised as a joke disguised as a peace offering disguised as nostalgia. Eli's message is clear. You would need a barometer to measure what you'd become from what you'd wanted to. It might be funny if you hadn't had to take off work, offload the kid on the ex, kennel the dog, if you weren't jet-lagged and sweaty. It might be revelatory if the objects had been selected with greater care and less spite. If they made sense.

Eli is the only one willing to investigate the mess of black feathers that, mashed against the inside of the canister, had been the first sign of wrongness. A chimera of a chimera: body of a deer mouse, wings of a cowbird. Both eyes are stitched shut with an X. Eli turns back to the three of you. He looks frightened, or older. He wears the expression of a person who, unlike his friends, has no explanation at which to arrive.

"My contribution was the handle of a canoe paddle. I broke it shooting rapids, whittled it into a bear."

Paul squats down and picks up a rusty railroad spike that some impressive force had torqued into a corkscrew. "Mine was my first homerun ball." There's a Polaroid on the ground. "Whoa," he laughs a laugh that has nothing to do with funniness. "Why do I get two?"

The photograph is of a teenage Paul, naked, seated on a bed.

Sheryl kneels and takes the photograph from him. "It's not yours. Don't you recognize that bedroom?"

Now it's Paul who has no explanation. "But . . . that never happened."

"No," Sheryl replies. "And my contribution was a mix tape of love songs."

Eli hands you a scroll of stapled pages that are too white for the years that have passed. "Yours?"

You remember contributing a short story you'd written, back when you assumed you'd be doing book tours by now. You read: *Unlike everything else from childhood, it's bigger than I remembered.*

You wrote them during class pretending to take notes. Voracious, wolfing stories. Stories that ignored precedent, devoured predecessors. Back before the authorities cited baffling examples to prove new ideas were done for. Before you learned, learned to polish the kind of annual gems that assure smart friends you're safe, subdued.

"Another thing bothers me," Paul says. "We know which object is ours."

A door opens, the back door of the house, and a woman steps out onto the deck. You suddenly remember that you're standing in someone's yard. Dressed like an Easter egg, she's as anonymous as the property's vinyl siding or gazing ball or Little Tikes play place or never-used hammock.

Four adults standing in her backyard near a hole. The explanation would have been quite reasonable—charming even—if not for what you had unearthed. She will want to know the same thing you're all currently wondering: What type of children had you been? She steps down into the grass and approaches the group.

Just as you're about to offer an explanation, she smiles at Eli and kisses him on the cheek.

You turn to the last page of your story hoping for an explanation. Paul and Sheryl crowd over your shoulders.

Eli's wedding ring, his smile of concession, his string of progeny that bang back open the door and rush to swarm the strangers.

There aren't that many of them, but they're impossible to count. Five? Five. One of the girls upends the slimy basin of a birdbath.

But Eli's not smiling. The surprise wasn't supposed to have been the time capsule.

The children seize upon the canister and hoist it above their heads like slain prey. Singing a song about one-way streets that is either brand-new or ancient, they carry the trophy toward the tangled undergrowth that is the property's backmost curtain.

"I want to call after them," Sheryl reads your narration, *"but who am I to give advice?"*

It's not one of them carries the capsule, but each lends a hand. It's twice as big as before, big enough to put your head into, swallowed by what wilds remain.

Is it in you?

From what our sources tell us, it isn't. At least not in sufficiently detectable amounts. We're pretty sure that it has been in you at some point—you're American, it's American. We want to put it back into you. Try to revive the bluffs that loomed above the outfield fence at Talcott-Page, the baseball-swallowing darkness that pocked the sumac and crevasses, the sirens—a gunshot once in a while—that reminded you this was the bad part of Rockford. As if you could have forgotten. It was summer and it was baseball and you were young, but dusk and storm clouds and the earthy smell of lightless culverts was an encounter with the end of something, there at the beginning.

Take a sip of Riptide Rush. Put Fierce Grape into you. Try to trick your body into believing—just for a moment—that you are still an athlete. That you still have it in you. Still need it in you.

Cover the Earth

Thank you valued customer. That is correct, a gallon of Sherwin-Williams Duration covers approximately 350 to 450 square feet depending on the surface and how thickly you apply it. Thank you valued customer. A Google search of the earth's square footage shows that your estimate is correct, about 5.5 quadrillion. Thank you valued customer. One hundred fifty years of sales records fail to produce a precise answer to your question. We doubt that we have sold 16 trillion gallons of paint. We have work to do. You have work to do. We ask you to be patient and take into account that we've covered lots of the earth with multiple coats. Take some 80 grit to your bedroom wall, the smaller bedroom: Forward Fuchsia, Casa Blanca, Underseas. What were they thinking? Thank you valued customer. Certainly the oceans present a problem, but painting your sister's house last night you poured perhaps a quarter quart down the sink rather than saving it. Only a tiny fraction of our oceans is paint. Only a tiny fraction of our oceans is fish.

Thank you, thank you, thank you valued customer. Every purchase you make, every fresh start, one gallon closer to keeping our promise.

Put a Tiger in your Tank

I was done and you were also apparently done and you were surprised to find that there was still a tiger in my tank. I curled into a fetal position, the spooned spoon, to conceal the tiger still in my tank, but your hand found a way through and you asked, Why do you still have a tiger in your tank? I put a tiger in my tank, I saw no way around admitting. Why would a young man still clinging to his twenties feel the need to put a tiger in his tank? You were angry, you were hurt, you were feeling unsexy. You don't understand. I knew you'd want to get drunk and open all our zoo cages, and sometimes when I put whiskey in my tank, the tiger leaves my tank after twenty minutes. I excuse myself to the den, I try to coax it back, I remind myself, You love naked women. Remember ten years ago when you'd enter my tank unbidden? When I'd have to walk from class to class coolly holding a binder over my jungle just to conceal that there was a tiger in my tank? I considered fake drinking tonight, but that seemed rapey. A guy at work had back pills and another coworker took one and said it put a tiger in his tank for four hours.

So, it's not you. It's this: the tiger knows our eldest should be feeling their first growls by now—and we should be winding down.

Ten Million Worldmarks
for the Ouroborics

When the first image appears on my screen and it's just a woman's hand with mauve fingernails peeling a banana, I think: This is going to be simple. Especially because one of the contestants, Redmund, had gotten agitated right away, simply from being unclad in front of the cameras and audience. That leaves just five of us.

"Our little twink is looking kind of arrogant," Jamson Tuscany, the host of NABCBS's *Find Your Fetish*, seems to read my mind.

He cues the audience like he's conducting a symphony, and they nail their entrance: "DON'T GET COCKY!"

Strutting around the stage and up into the aisles, Jamson Tuscany isn't wearing much more than the contestants are, just underwear sequined with emeralds and a big peacock tail. From the neck up he appears female, with long blond hair and eyelashes like Venus flytraps.

Above the banana, which is now being inserted into an *O* of sizable glistening lips the same color as the fingernails, are video feeds of my fellow remaining contestants: Angela, Sisu, Skeldon, and Mikiki. Redmund's feed is now a static image, a fresco of Priapus with a very sizable and agitated urinator. Through my earpiece, I hear a female voice going *Mmmm Mmmmmm MMMmmmmmm!* like the banana tastes better than any other banana has ever tasted before. The other contestants appear to be equally at peace with whatever images they're being shown—it might be the banana, I'm not sure—but I tell myself that spending too much time glancing at their uncladness is probably not going to help me win ten million worldmarks for the Ouroborics.

Stop, I tell myself. You shouldn't be thinking words such as *unclad*—

No, don't, not even to evict it from your mind. Nor *shaved* nor *ankles* nor *mammaries*—

Enough. Remember Father Terroy's sage advice, "Focus is forgotten at the moment of its reminder." Shouldn't be anticipating the ten million either. Instead, Father Terroy quoting the mystic Randy: "*To each his own agitation. What's weird for one's the world of another.*" Eyes off the prize.

Could they be reading my mind? Because now an image of the prize money appears on the screen, a messy pile of tidy stacks like they used in the old days. The studio audience oohs and ahs and claps and whistles, seeing the same image projected on a larger screen above my head. The house lights are dim, but I can discern their featureless faces in my peripheral vision. I have to tilt my head up to see my smaller screen, located at a height so that it won't block my uncladness from the scrutiny of the audience and cameras. On the screen now, a showy man in dress clothes sipping an amber-colored drink from a stubby tumbler, plus two women whose dress clothes reveal their sizable mammar—

Stop. Two showy women is all, red lips and fingernails, hanging on to the man's shoulders as he throws dice down a green felt table. Over my earpiece, a woman sings, "*She raunch a sleaze with lotto marks, not some little drip.*" If I were to turn my head to the left or right, I would see Skeldon and Sisu, but I would be immediately disqualified for averting my eyes from the screen. Now the man is on a yacht, wind-buffeted, watching the sun plunge into a tranquil sea. "*He coffs her aquifers, she hails him sparky. She hails me little drip.*"

These agitations are not my agitations. I'm content knowing that my parents have promised to tithe a good portion of my winnings to the Order of Ouroborics in payment for my years of training. Content knowing that the fruit of my victory will help them spread True Solipsism and the Wisdom of Randy to parts of this world still rife with coupling and community.

The screen gives up trying to agitate me with earthly riches. Feet squelch in bubbling mud for a minute, are rinsed clean. Fingers interlace the toes like heathen prayer. Now the close-up of a bellybutton, a female's I believe, as it is squirted with pale liquid. I'm not sure how this is supposed to agitate me. The liquid beads on the skin, shiny and viscous. A hand appears, rubbing the liquid around on the skin, pushing it down into the bellybutton. I resist the urge to survey my own body, gauge the visibility of the surgical scars on my chest in the bright, bright stage lights.

The sound of one ding notifies the contestants and the audience and the viewers at home that someone is starting to get agitated. I look at the feeds of my fellow contestants. It's Angela. The cartoon flower at the bottom right corner of her screen, previously just a bud, has started to bloom.

Brother Jehrem explained to me that the physiological effects of agitation in the female human are less obvious to viewers, and so they must be hooked up to a scientific device. I don't know how the device works, but with each ding it drizzles perfumed liquid onto the stage floor.

"Here at NABCBS's *Find Your Fetish* . . . ," Jamson Tuscany croons.

"EVERYONE—" but the crowd's distinct words are obscured by their polyphony.

I was told that he's the fourth Jamson Tuscany in the history of *Find Your Fetish*, that he too will be replaced when he turns twenty-six.

The perfume permeating the studio is not an odor I can readily identify as pleasant: vanilla, sandalwood, myrrh, Brother Gorf's pipe tobacco. Nor my favorite flowers that bloom in the abbey garden: sweet peas, alyssum, lily of the valley, four-o'clocks. Nor my favorite foods: bacon, raspberry jam, cornbread, Brother Jim's sugar rolls straight out of the oven. It's *almost* a bad smell—but I want to keep smelling it. Brother Caffey warned me that agitating language was being purposefully withheld from me as part of my training, and I'm suddenly sure that those expurgated words possess the means of describing this perfume. I'd taken Brother Caffey's revelation as joyous news, knowing it gave me an advantage over my worldly fellow contestants—but suddenly it leaves me feeling a little scooped out, like this turtle I once saw trying to crawl beneath a fence. He couldn't squeeze under because of his shell, but the invisible obstacle didn't stop him from trying and trying and trying.

On the screen now, two horses are conceiving a foal. The male horse is amazingly agitated, its urinator sizable as it mounts the willing filly from behind. Conditions seem auspicious for the creation of new life!

My teachers at the Order don't know it, but I'm not wholly inexperienced when it comes to conceiving with horses. Once I came across my filly, Dardanel, conceiving with a stallion that had apparently—so said my friend Myatt—been brought to the abbey grounds for that express purpose. Dardanel is my horse—I used to ride her every day after morning calisthenics—and seeing this stranger horse with her was the first time I ever became agitated aside from the agitation brought about by the treachery of nighttime dreams. I became agitated again the next morning as I rode Dardanel harder than usual. The producers of *Find Your Fetish* conduct extensive interviews with each contestant prior to filming so that they can curate the agitating material specifically for our unique appetites—but I didn't mention the verboten Dardanel memory at all during the interview, only that I have a horse named Dardanel and I used to ride her every single day after morning calisthenics. To maintain peace of body I take deep breaths and try to recall every step of my favorite hike, up the mountain vale to the spring that is the origin of the Bitterroot Falls. And ward off agitation with the simple Wisdom of Randy: *The only worthwhile travel is the journey into oneself.* Blessed truth!

My fellow contestants are the usual mix of ages and skin colors. Mikiki is from Recife, Brazil, and is about the same age as me. I know this because Jamson Tuscany read off our profiles as each one of us walked onto the stage, spotlighted and unclad. Skeldon is an American like me but a few years older, twenty. He has corrupted his pure skin with several tattoos. Redmund, Sisu, and Angela are all older, in their twenties and early thirties. Redmund was Nambian. *Is*, I correct myself. He's not going home with ten million worldmarks, but it's not like he's dead! Sisu is from Helsinki, Russia, and she's the one whose ankles I really better not dally upon because she's so showy. Even just her name, how the first syllable demands you look at her. *Seeeee*-su. And look, and look, and keep looking forever. We're all very showy people. Very seldom do they let someone of humble appearance or advanced age onto *Find Your Fetish*, for obvious reasons. When they do, you always know it's a joke.

Or that's what I've heard, at least. There are various philosophies on how best to maintain one's peace of body on *Find Your Fetish*, and my trainers subscribe to the idea that the most severe abstention from agitating material will produce a contestant who has the tightest control over himself. So I was forbidden from ever watching a single episode, though Father Terroy did describe the show's premise to me at some length.

Skeldon, the only other remaining male contestant, was reared under a polar-opposite philosophy. Skeldon's parents own Lake Huron, enabling them to dedicate sizable resources to his training. In his introduction, Jamson Tuscany, using many words that are unfamiliar to me, described how Skeldon had been shown agitating materials eight hours a day from a very early age. Once he'd reached the stage of development at which bodily agitation becomes possible, he'd conceived daily with both females and males, sometimes groups of them. His descendants must outnumber the stars! Until spotlighted Skeldon was introduced, I did not know that males could conceive with other males, and I'm still trying to figure out what could be gained from such a coupling. The act could not yield new life under even the most auspicious circumstances. *You know why*, the words pop into my head, and I'm surprised not to hear my first ding.

The only true baptism is at thine own font, I remind myself.

I need to be more careful.

In fact, Jamson told the crowd, Skeldon's quarantine (the three days leading up to showtime during which we were kept under continual surveillance so we couldn't "masturbate") was the first time in over five years he'd gone a day without conceiving children or masturbating. Of course the quarantine was no problem for me—that's been my life so far.

A ding.

For me. Corruption!

No mistake. I'm feeling agitated down there. Why?

"Whoa, hold my horses!" Jamson Tuscany booms. "Our sweet little twink is having trouble controlling himself!"

It's *not horses*. Then what?

It's masturbate. Somehow I know what it means, and I feel myself notch closer to adulthood. That's growing up: the continual pummeling of joy and regret every time you learn there's a word for something you thought was your own personal discovery. But masturbate is the wrong word, too brainy and scientific. Masturbate is Father Kwintz reading a big dusty book, or showing me how to invalidate a competitor's argument using logic.

That's one of the regrets, when a word hides the thing or action it's supposed to reveal. Because don't they call out to us, radiate their true selves, beg us to use our species-specific gift to choose the perfect name forevermore? *Mud*, or *dwindle*, or *clip-clop*, or *susurrus*. To think that my brethren would feel this rutting itch long ago and collectively decide on—

No. Stop it. Minutes ago *unclad* and *ankles* risked agitation— how far I've fallen! Return to your Randy, wayward backslider. *Original sin was the first time humans made eye contact.*

In the bottom right of my screen, the mercury in a thermometer the shape of a urinator is rising. Everyone in the audience is making noise, and I wonder for the first time if they're struggling to maintain peace of body. Or not. Not struggling but just letting themselves become agitated. I imagine a little engorged thermometer or obscene flower floating over each of their dark faces.

Tuscany: "I've always questioned the wisdom of nominating a contestant who's at the age he'd fuck a hole in the wall."

He who drinks of himself shall live forever.

I think of my parents and my sister watching at home, biting their hands in nervousness. I think of Father Terroy and Brother

Caffey and Brother Skofield and Brother Zev and Brother Gwayne and everyone else breaking their vow against TV just to cheer me on. I will not be taking ten million worldmarks back to them, but I'll still bring in five if I can restrain myself from here on out.

Jamson Tuscany deals a kettledrum one hard whack and pedals a glissando, signifying peace of body. The drum is printed with an advertisement for buckets of fried chicken.

"Saved by the limp timpani. Time for our studio audience and you viewers at home to send in your votes for the exact type of titillation you want inflicted on our meek and innocent contestants in round two. That's right, I'll see you right back here for our famous . . ."

"REACH-A-ROUND!"

We have been fitted with glasses that allow us to view the screens but prevent us from identifying the object or anticipating when and where it will contact our showy bodies, like Dardanel's blinders on the few occasions I was allowed to ride her into town, chaperoned, except blinding us below rather than to the sides.

Skeldon dings once just in anticipation, and I admit that I'm anxious to find out what the viewers have chosen for me.

Left thigh! Tickly! I laugh, causing the audience to laugh, but grow no more agitated than before.

Sisu dings even though I can see on her screen that the ice cubes haven't yet made contact with her skin, and I almost ding again thinking it's my laughter that's caused her to become agitated.

Focus is forgotten at the moment of its reminder.

Although Sisu had no official training for *Find Your Fetish*, Jamson Tuscany had quoted her boast during the intros—that she'd seen enough carnage and tragedy during her military tours in the

Reign of Error to gird her against any and all future pleasure. She flinches as the ice cubes begin their path from the valley below her throat through the canyon between her mammaries, and I can tell she's unsure for one second whether the sensation is hot or cold.

You preserve vital life force when you make of your body a closed circuit.

I can't see myself on the screen, but I've already identified my object, which is now traveling the opposite path of Sisu's ice cubes, up my chest, eventually to my chin. I've been swatted enough by Dardanel's coquettish tail to know horsehair when I feel it on my skin. Skeldon is further tattooed brown and white and red from chocolate sauce and whipped cream and maraschino cherries, Angela goosebumped but so far not agitated by the defanged cobras exploring her shins and shoulders, Mikiki weirdly being subjected to a dull knife tracing her aureoles, a rope around her neck, choking her lightly.

Angela screams, dings, as one of the snakes flicks its forked tongue into her ear.

The horsetail dodges my urinator to continue down my other leg and sweep around my toes. *The young must always aid those elders whose muscles have betrayed them.* Brother Jehrem told me that there was no way to know what I could expect in the Reach-A-Round, but that the rules strictly forbade genital contact.

Jamson Tuscany sounds the fried chicken kettledrum again. "I've beat my meat, folks—now you have a chance to do the same. Rub one off to Chuckin Drum's Meat Bones and our other proud sponsors, and we'll see you right back here for round three . . ."

"THE ALL-OUT SEX BOUT."

* * *

Our eyes leave the screens for the first time since the introductions, directed to the now-crowded stage front where various showy strangers have assembled themselves around three mattresses, a wrestling mat, and a Twister game pad.

Most of them are unclad, though two of the males are wearing wrestling outfits and one woman is terrifying in black plastic and heels. I have been appointed a trio of showy young people, two males and one female. They begin pecking one another alternately and embracing.

"For Angela," Jamson Tuscany announces, "two new initiates at the most exclusive sorority on campus, ordered to play a naked game of Twister by their twisted sisters. Skeldon has seen it all, except maybe real love. We scoured the world for a husband and wife who seem to actually like each other. He's unprotected, she's ovulating, and tonight they're trying to conceive their fourth child right here on air. We thought we might tempt our chilly Finn with two boys at wrestling camp trying as hard as they can to disguise their sport's obvious front for homoerotic play. No safe word for Mikiki as she's shown exactly how Frau Petra von Schlangenkampf raunches a very naughty banking sleaze. We didn't know *what* to do for our uncut little twink, so we'll let him decide for himself."

Skeldon, the dessert ingredients cleaned off him, yawns at the loving couple's tender attempts to procreate.

The female in my trio is now lying on her back, and one of the showy males is conceiving with her. I wonder what the other male's going to—

Debased! He mounts the other male in the manner of a stallion!

Muscle cramps are the future gift for the insatiable hunger of now, I remind myself, not sure if I'm in need of calming or not.

Angela triple dings and is eliminated.

"Right hand on red, and both feet off my stage! We're down to four, folks!"

As far as I know, Angela was—*is*—just a normal person with no special training. They always have a few of these types on *Find Your Fetish*.

"It looks like Sisu's wrestlers have given up the act, are now coupling in their singlets. Blue just checked Red's oil!"

Sisu dings a second time, and I ding a second time, more in response to her ding than the confusing sex bout happening on the mattress before me. Another four million worldmarks, forfeited!

Consume your bounty, or choke on munificence, I ticker-tape Randy through my mind. ~~Sisu's thin ankles~~ *We shall be likened to subsistence farmers of our own fecundity.* ~~Skeldon's narrow hips~~ *Don't do unto others; do unto thyself.*

I feel great warmth for Sisu. I imagine her the figurehead on the prow of a ship I'm sailing. (I'm captain of the ship.)

"Slow down, kids—it's a twenty-four-hour news cycle!" Jamson Tuscany beats his meat again, whatever that means. "We better send off our wrestlers and sorority sisters, our young libertines and our lifers, our lovely Frau Petra von Schlangenkampf and her battered CEO. To them we say . . ."

"GO GET A ROOM!"

My trio disengages, suddenly strangers.

"When we come back, our contestants go back on the *offensive*"—he pronounces offensive like the adjective, synonym to corrupt or debased or deviant—"right back here on NABCBS's . . ."

"FIND YOUR FETISH!"

Our screens have left their perches and alighted within a foot of our faces so we can select the agitating material with which we want to "libido torpedo" a fellow contestant. I thrill at the idea of agitating Sisu, but I also don't want to see her booted off the stage just yet. So I go after Mikiki instead. The screen is divided into a seven-by-ten grid, and I don't know what half the options mean. I know I'm allowed to mix and match, but I'm having trouble even choosing one. *Amputees? Self-sucking? Furries? Shit and piss?* Corrupt! Maybe *Vampires*. Because I at least know what a vampire is. And I enjoy gothic stories about them, the spookier the better, in particular the famous tale of Volusian, the vampire so pure and ethical that he learned to survive by biting his own wrist. I jab my finger toward *Vampires*, but I'm feeling so disembodied by my recitation from Randy's *Narcissus Unlimited* during the commercial break that I miscalculate and select *Violence* instead. Oh no, poor Mikiki!

Our screens pull back, and immediately a person in a horse costume trots into a photoreal pasture, walking erect like a human. Why is everyone so obsessed with horses today! A second person in a quadruped horse costume—actually, that must be *two* people—approaches the first. They begin to nuzzle—

Mikiki dings. Double dings!

"Get out your umbrellas, folks!"

During the introductions, Jamson Tuscany had described Mikiki's rigorous training as "Pavlovian." Apparently, like Skeldon, she was presented all throughout her youth with an excess of agitating material, but her body's agitated response would be met with painful consequences such as electric shock and nausea and jazz.

When a contestant suffers two dings, their feed on all of the other contestants' screens switches to show whatever content the agitated person is viewing. I say goodbye to my horses temporarily and gag at what replaces the feed of Mikiki. I'm more in danger of vomiting than agitation. The bellybutton is back, but now a black-gloved hand is slicing cryptic glyphs into the skin with a very sharp knife. The feed cuts back to Mikiki's scrawny body, shaking, convulsing almost, as she struggles to keep her eyes on her screen. Screams through my earpiece, rising excitement from the studio audience. I guess it's true—what's weird for one is the world for another.

The knife stops momentarily at the bellybutton—then plunges in up to the hilt!

Three dings. Mikiki is gone. Perfume permeates the auditorium, and she is carried off the stage in tears.

"Watch out, folks! There's some real sickos out there!" Jamson Tuscany holds out his hands like icons of Randy. "Three left . . ."

Our screens descend again, and I notice that three new libido torpedo squares have appeared: *Sisu*, *Skeldon*, and one with my name. *Bestiality*? *Bukkake*? How would *Language* and *Soccer Cleats* manifest themselves as agitating material? And what would sending *myself* to Sisu or Skeldon as agitating material look like? I realize I'm taking too much time, that the other contestants have already made their selections and the audience is becoming increasingly agitated. Not in *that* way . . .

"Hurry up, twink," a gruff voice that isn't Jamson Tuscany says through my earpiece.

I select Skeldon as the recipient, and then, almost at random, *Parental Love*.

Sisu's face, or a photoreal simulation of it, appears on my screen. Through my earpiece, her exotic Russian voice: "You've been so alone, Logo, your whole life." Hearing my name from her photoreal mouth is almost enough to send me packing. "You were raised by thieves. Sensations were stolen from you at the very moment you were becoming aware of their existence . . ." *A body at peace is a load released.* My eyes drift up to the feed of the real Sisu, whose face is betraying her mounting agitation. I become convinced that Skeldon sent her a photoreal simulation of himself, plus soccer cleats.

Skeldon double-dings, as if in affirmation.

On his feed, Skeldon is replaced by a man tickling a boy affectionately. Father and son playfulness. The video makes me feel something—Brother Jehrem promised that I will be granted visitation rights to see Mother and Father if I win the worldmarks—but what I feel is not genital agitation. Again, scooped out. A woman enters, pointing at a piece of paper and speaking in another language. I don't understand it, but the woman is obviously very pleased. She pets her son on the head—

Skeldon reappears on his feed, having regained his peace of body.

Photoreal me walks unclad onto my screen, steps into a tub of steaming water. Sisu takes off her clothes. *Observe the dog chasing his tail. The dog knows.* She kneels down beside the tub and begins to bathe me with a bar of soap and gobletfuls of warm water. "Logo, my wounded, gelded little foal, you are not broken. I will heal you, teach you." The tub becomes see-through, so I can observe her hand moving down my chest. *At the moment of tip touching tip, the penitent achieves ultimate freedom: absolute self-sufficiency.* "You've been hearing lots of words this past week that make no sense to you. This is your penis. Better yet, this is your cock." On the screen, my cock becomes agitated. "Hard," Sisu corrects me. *Two people, by necessity, can be ouroboric.* "Better than masturbate, you can beat your meat. You can jack off."

Jack off.

Lo, the act has found its adequate abstraction.

What happens when they botch the names, those bumbling long-gone Adams, is that years and years and centuries of humans reject the stone-inscribed cognomen, try out new monikers in secret, more of a continuous beveling than the light bulb *a-ha* that just flattened me. The true name destroys the official name, rust-like, until despite the greater diversity of words, we all will speak the same language in time.

The phrase "jack off" *is* jacking off. I want to be a clerk tasked with transcribing holy writ, but who instead writes *jack off* over and over and over.

No, there might be a still more perfect name than *jack off* somewhere in the ether. And isn't that an even more scary and enthralling prospect? What if I were the one to discover it?

Language never arrives.

Words don't mean what they mean, Father Kwintz. Words mean what they've come to mean—

No! Words mean what *they're coming* to mean. Always.

Sisu triple dings and disappears from the stage, from my screen, from my life. Perfume, her dissipating ghost.

The hermit is a man flexible enough to require only himself, some wilting inner habit lashes out in desperation. *We must reimagine St. Michael the snake.*

She's replaced by photoreal Skeldon, tattoos and all. "I'm jealous of all the innocence you get to lose, Logo. Another secret: Have you ever wondered why the Order's symbol is a snake biting its own tail?" He's finished drying me off, and we're sitting unclad on a couch together. *Circumcision is shortcoming.* "Have you ever questioned the morning calisthenics? I'm sure you can do it too, if you try." Skeldon leans close enough for me to read his skin, positioning a pillow behind my back. Photoreal me pulls his right leg back over his head.

"The Ouroborics prefer the term 'auto-fellatio.'"

Wrong word.

From Adam's rib was born Eve. By giving our ribs we correct the mistake.

Skeldon traces my photoreal surgical scars. "Self. Sucking."

I've lost the worldmarks. I'm done. Not because of any sight or sound or smell—

I ding three times.

"Hanged like a horse, our twink has found his fetish!"

It's the words.

All these new words, illicit and teeming.

Game in the Sand

They have finished securing Karl to the hood of the Chevy using the collected belts of everyone involved in production. Karl is unsure of many things. If his reflection will be visible in the windshield. If it will be obvious how slowly they're driving the truck. If he can slip through the harness they've rigged. If a cop will drive by and call cut. Don't drop the camera, Ernst wishes him luck. Couldn't you just steal another one? As if sensing the cameraman's discomfort, Lukas (Alrick) botches his single line. Peter (Uwe) somehow botches hearing it.

FADE IN:

INT. TRUCK — DAY

ALRICK BERLING (25) is driving the beat-up truck. His father UWE (50) is in the passenger seat. Through the windows, rolling sand dunes. Twangy COUNTRY MUSIC plays on the radio, almost inaudible.

Alrick is dressed in a style that might be called "business beach," with a pastel button-down shirt tucked into khakis. On his feet, boat shoes. His hair is blond and

neatly styled. His attractive face is set and
humorless, his gaze unwavering.

Uwe wears an old trucker hat and a pearl-button
shirt with epaulets, cowboy boots on his feet,
a pack of cigarettes in his front pocket. His
hair is salt-and-pepper, his cheeks coarse with
stubble. His face is pocked, maybe scarred, his
eyes dark.

Uwe has some sort of mental disorder, like
one that might result from a head trauma. He
doesn't speak strangely, just slowly, and he's
slow to process information. He nods his head
too often and seems to have little control
over his fingers when they're not holding
a cigarette.

Alrick turns off the RADIO.

                    ALRICK
          You have to promise not to
          overreact.

EXT. ROAD — MOMENTS LATER

The truck SWERVES suddenly, comes to an abrupt
stop on the side of the road.

Can you tell there's no dog in the back of the truck? Ernst wants to know. Should we go get the dog? Karl says no to the first, yes to the second. The angle is such that you can't see the bed. But we've left that dog too long. If someone comes across it— It'll be fine, Ernst insists. At least go check on the guys, Karl says. I bet they got thrown around in there a little bit.

INT. TRUCK — CONTINUOUS

Uwe is behaving childishly, sobbing to himself as he holds his knees to his chest and rocks back and forth.

Alrick rubs his jaw. His appraisal of his father is disgusted but not angry. He antici-pated this scene and is not surprised by it.

              ALRICK
   Now's the time for courage. You
   have to be a man.

Uwe presses himself against the passenger-side door, trying to get as far away from his son as possible. Hatred is in his eyes.

           ALRICK (CONT'D)
   Courage means doing what's right,
   what's kind, even when it seems
   like unkindness. I've been
   dreading this trip for weeks, but

     it can't wait any longer. ~~It's~~
     ~~time.~~

INT. TRUCK — MINUTES LATER

They are driving again, but in a heavy silence.
Uwe has turned his shoulder to his son. This
brooding stretches out for an uncomfortable
length of time.

The dog is still there when they return to the unofficial access
point of the dunes and the sea beyond them. Leashed to a tree,
the dog tries to jump joyfully at the return of its abandoners. But
its old age and feebleness show, qualities that Ernst had insisted
upon. The dog's owner was originally supposed to accompany them
on the shoot as "Animal Wrangler," but had canceled last minute,
entrusting the dog to Peter. Despite its advanced age, the dog keeps
disobeying the script and leaping from the bed of the truck every
time Peter opens the hatch. Peter is forced to light cigarette after
cigarette, exacerbating the tension between him and Ernst.

INT./EXT. TRUCK/PARKING AREA — MINUTES LATER

The pair arrive at their destination. The
parking area is wayward and overgrown with
tufts of grass sprouting through what may or
may not be a patch of asphalt. No other cars
are present.

Uwe, now smoking a CIGARETTE, walks around to
the bed of the truck, in which there's a DOG,
wagging its tail excitedly. Uwe lets down the
hatch, but the dog is too old to jump down by
itself. Uwe has to pick it up and set it on
the ground.

Alrick produces a SHOTGUN from behind the seats
of the truck.

He walks around to the back of the truck where
Uwe is playing with the dog. He gets a SHOVEL
out of the bed.

>   ALRICK
>   Let's go.

He begins to walk toward the dunes, but neither
Uwe nor the dog follow him. Alrick notices,
turns, and steps toward them. The dog cowers.

Alrick sees the predicament he's in. The dog
won't follow him.

>   ALRICK (CONT'D)
>   Dog never liked me.

>   UWE
>   He knows why we're here. ~~Somehow.~~

> ALRICK

He's not going to come unless you
lead.

Uwe sadly considers. His son grows impatient.

> ALRICK (CONT'D)

The trip's for him, remember. And
for you. It wasn't easy for me to
get this time off work.
> (pause)

Or I can shoot him here.

> UWE

Someone might drive by. ~~Might see.~~

> ALRICK

It's no crime to kill a cancerous
old dog.

The logistical problem, as Karl had warned Ernst, is that the dog
will follow Lukas—won't *not* follow him, that is. Ernst eventually
cracks a joke about nailing the dog's ass to the asphalt, and Peter
takes offense. Ernst tells Peter to save the drama for the scene,
where he could use a little more of it. Lukas begins complaining
again about the dialogue, that it still feels too leading and stilted,
causing Ernst to launch into one of his by-now-famous sermons
about how the scene has moved into stylized unreality and that

we must not think as humans think. How he has no desire for collaborators, only co-conspirators.

EXT. DUNES — MINUTES LATER

The trio are walking along the dunes, Uwe between his son and the dog.

> UWE
>
> This is the right place. We had such wonderful holidays here.

> ALRICK
>
> Remember when I was training for football and I would run up and down the Pyramid?

> UWE
>
> I tried to run with you--so did
>
> _____.

He looks down at the dog. The dog's name is

_____.

> UWE (CONT'D)
>
> But I'd only make it about halfway up. I'm afraid those days are behind us, for _____ and for me.

                    ALRICK

Mom would make sandwiches and
potato salad.

                     UWE

I wish she was here. She'd be able
to help take care of _____ and we
wouldn't have to do this.

                    ALRICK

I think you're right. But we can't
uncrash her plane.

Uwe is struggling more and more visibly with
his emotions now. But he's no longer thinking
of the dog.

                     UWE

~~How come we couldn't have a funeral
for her? Buy her a tombstone
at least?~~

                    ALRICK

~~I've told you this. Her body was
lost.~~

                     UWE

~~But~~ don't they sometimes have
funerals when there's no body?
What about soldiers?

> ALRICK
>
> ~~Soldiers are different. Those~~
> ~~aren't real funerals, anyway.~~
> Those are memorials~~, cenotaphs~~.

Alrick picks up a piece of driftwood lying in
the sand. He tries to hand it to his father.

> ALRICK (CONT'D)
> Fetch?

Uwe looks sickened. He shakes his head.

From recollecting the past, Alrick is showing
his first emotions so far. It should be clear,
however, and not too subtly, that this is
rather mediocre melodramatic acting.

> ALRICK (CONT'D)
> We're coming to the end. Throw the
> stick for _____. Let him remember
> for a moment what it was like to be
> a young dog ~~here on holiday~~.

This display of emotion seems to win over Uwe.
He sees a sympathetic side to his son. They
have made a connection.

Uwe nods and takes the stick. He waves it in
front of the disinterested dog.

> UWE

Fetch, _____?

He throws the stick.

The dog watches the stick but makes no attempt to run after it.

> UWE (CONT'D)

Go get it. Go get it, boy.

The dog lopes off in the direction of the stick. He picks it up and brings it back to the father.

Ernst takes over control of the Arri, and Karl is trying to hide his resentment. Ernst has set up the Sony at a side angle and tells Karl to keep him and the Arri in frame and to leave the Sony running until he says cut. Egomaniac that he is, the crew has no difficulty believing that Ernst is making his own making-of. With a crew of just four, there's no one to capture sound now, and Ernst is left holding the boom in the crux of his elbow. He says the heat is degrading the celluloid and he wants to get this scene in one shot. Are you ready to cry? he asks Peter. Peter is ready to glare.

EXT. DUNES — MINUTES LATER

The three are standing still, Alrick across from Uwe and the dog, who are side by side.

                    UWE
        I'll do it. He's my dog, so it's
        my job.

                    ALRICK
        Your eyes aren't good anymore, and
        your hands shake. If you don't hit
        him perfectly, he'll suffer ~~before~~
        ~~dying~~.

Uwe considers, then nods.

                    ALRICK (CONT'D)
        Any last words?

Uwe is fighting his tears and losing.

                    UWE
        He was a good dog. He was loyal
        and he never complained, even when
        he got old and weak and we had to
        give him medicine. Was it his
        fault he got sick? No, it's just
        what happens to an old dog.

Alrick points the gun at the dog. Then he raises
it up and shoots his father in the chest.

The dog BARKS and Uwe falls to the ground. The
dog stands above him as he convulses for a few

seconds before dying. At the end, he seems to
try to reach up with one hand, either to the
dog or his son.

Alrick is breathing hard. He stands there
holding the gun for an uncomfortable length of
time, as much as eight whole seconds. Finally,
he looks at the camera--or just above, rather.

Ernst keeps his eye to the camera and says nothing. What a bang!
Lukas laughs. So real. With his foot he nudges Peter, still lying on
the ground and being attended to by the dog. Alright Peter, Lukas
says, I'm saying cut. The smile leaves Lukas's face. He realizes that
there was a live round in the gun and that he has killed Peter. This
should not be too dramatic.

INT. VAN — DAY (FLASHBACK)

Ernst is driving the van, Peter in the
passenger seat. Lukas and Karl are not in the
car but are following them in the truck. Peter,
of course, is not in character, so he no longer
acts mentally impaired.

Both Ernst and Peter are pissed. They are in
the middle of an argument.

                    PETER
     You go too far, Ernst. Once again.

> ERNST

The Academy never lets anyone use it. Once a year it gets brought out of the equipment closet. But the door was open and I knew it wasn't even theft, knew that I had a right to it. The films I make will justify the act.

> PETER

It was theft. I'm not surprised. Piglets nursing from a dead sow. There's a word for that kind of filmmaking: snuff. The thing about snuff is that anybody can do it. It takes no talent, just badness.

> ERNST

What you call badness, I call guts. Should I turn the van around, now that we're three hours from home?

Peter considers.

> PETER

Because we've already invested so much, I'll help you finish it. But, after this film, I'm out.

                    ERNST
Yes, you're out.

                    PETER
And you're returning the camera when
we get back. That's my condition.

Do I actually have to point it at him? Lukas asked, examining the gun. Karl and Peter were unloading supplies from the van. If it was a side angle, the answer would be no, Ernst told him. But with the angle I'm planning, they'll be able to tell. Peter took the gun and checked the chambers. I don't like guns and I don't like having them pointed at me. Ernst held out his hand for the gun, and Peter gave it to him. Ernst pointed it at his own boot and pulled the trigger. A harmless click sounded. Do you think I'm completely stupid? He held up the blank so Peter could inspect it. Cover your ears, friends.

EXT. DUNES — DAY (RETURN TO PRESENT)

Back in the film "Game in the Sand," Lukas is
again the character Alrick, but it is obvious
that he is no longer acting. He is sweaty and
is breathing very hard, distraught over having
killed Peter. He no longer holds the gun.

Peter lies dead on the ground, and the dog is
WHINING over his body.

The entrance to the scene is messy, as it's
uncertain whether or not Lukas will pull
himself together to finish filming.

> DIRECTOR (O.C.)
> Pick up the shovel.

Lukas picks up the shovel but looks at it like
a technology happened upon in a science fiction
world.

> DIRECTOR (O.C.) (CONT'D)
> Start digging. About three feet to
> the left of his body.

He starts digging.

Ernst stands at the top of a tall dune, staring over the sea. Wind
moves through his hair and there's an ineffable depth to his gaze,
as if he can fathom farther horizons than most men. His demeanor
says, The die is cast. This moment of meditation should be that of
a prototypical Romantic mystic.

EXT. DUNES — DAY

A landscape of majestic dunes against a
stunning sky. Alrick and the dog can be seen
descending one dune, walking toward the camera.
Cue an ancient recording of Josquin's "Absolon

fili mi." (The oldest you can find. I want to *hear* the wax.) Alrick carries the shovel but not the gun.

MINUTES LATER

Alrick and the dog walk toward the parked truck. A posh sports car pulls up beside the truck. Alrick gets into the passenger side of the sports car.

The car pulls away.

Leave the dog behind.

FADE OUT.

Lucky Girl

VI.

Music so faint she mistakes it for thought.

Most mornings she forgets the songs she wrote the night before. Sometimes she salvages one and figures it out on her guitar, but the new song is usually so different that she can't trace it back to its spark. That's Dani's answer to friends who hint that her songwriting methods border on plagiarism. It's true that she controls the playlist, an ever-growing creature cobbled together of various genres. A creature named *Nepenthe*. She feeds it a glut of emblematic ballads. She tells it to shuffle, but it does the shuffling. Then she lies in bed and lets the sub-audible provoke the subconscious. The songs themselves are written by liminal delusion, by mishearing, by stillborn dreams.

This song . . . "Knocks Me Off My Feet"? No, not even close: Janet Jackson's "Come Back to Me." And, like every time she identifies a song, the composition she'd been flirting with vanishes. If she really wants any new material, she'll have to get up out of bed and turn down her computer speakers a microscopic degree. But that will set back her passage into sleep at least another ten minutes.

And she isn't getting much sleep these days—that's the main problem with her new job. At the slightest hallway noise, not to mention the late-night "emergency" knocks, her heart overcompensates. Then she has to decide whether or not to get up, to risk a draining argument with one of her students (ninety percent of the time Chelsea Bernadetti) about why their reasons for roaming the halls after lights-out are inadequate. Then another noise. Laughter. All the more irksome because they think they're getting away with it. She finds herself attentively awaiting just what she hopes not to hear.

The identified "Come Back to Me" concludes, and the next song is transformed by its low volume from something she's heard a million times, a track that once defined an August or October, into a catchy riddle of guitar and trumpet, three plus three plus two. She decides against flipping on her lamp and trying to jot it all down on staff paper—not because it isn't worth remembering, but rather because it's so distinct that she's sure she won't forget it tomorrow. And her first nonsensical thought of the night, the damp band between tide and dry sand: *Men will tear at their pretty little cages until they are free—*

A knock on her bedroom door.

What night is it? Tuesday or Wednesday, her days off? Can she ignore it?

No, it's Saturday, right in the middle of her nontraditional workweek. She rolls over and checks the red letters on her digital clock. Two forty-eight a.m. The second knock seems to be the actual muscles springing her out of bed as she throws on a T-shirt and some pajama pants. "Just a minute!"

Although she expects her prime drama queen, Arielle Hendry, or possibly some antics centered around Ms. Bernadetti, she's surprised to find Yoon-jee Ahn on her threshold, crying.

"Sorry, Dani, sorry," Yoon-jee whimpers, taking a few tiny shuffle steps toward the open door.

Annoyance is now impossible. Try being annoyed at Yoon-jee's bunny slippers or her pink pajamas covered in cartoon skulls and bombs with lit fuses.

"Yoon-jee, what's wrong?" Dani doesn't move from her position in the doorway.

The tiny girl glances right and left down the dorm hallway, whispers, "Can we talk please?"

"We can talk in the office downstairs."

"In your room?"

"Only if I prop the door open."

"Why?"

Explaining the residence life protocol is awkward, especially to an emotionally distraught, newly arrived international student. Dani concedes the doorway. "No big deal," she says, maybe mostly to herself, as just the windowlessness of the door enclosing her in a room with a student feels scandalous.

Dani pushes some clothes off of her couch and motions for Yoon-jee to sit down.

"Thank you, Dani," she says, not sitting down until Dani does.

"Would you like a drink? Some hot cocoa?"

"No thank you."

"Can you tell me what's bothering you?"

Yoon-jee hangs her head, shaking it back and forth for a moment. Her shoulders begin quivering.

"Yoon-jee . . ." Dani holds out a box of tissues.

Yoon-jee's arm is covered in doodles and writing, as if her peers had mistaken her skin for a fiberglass cast. Bo LaMott, the head of the visual arts department at Andermatt Arts Academy, has lately been on a crusade against such temporary tattoos, certain they are a gateway to cutting.

"Thank you, Dani." But a half minute passes and she says nothing more.

"Yoon-jee, I'm gonna have trouble helping if you don't tell me what's on your mind."

She continues to shake her head, covering her face with a tissue.

"Problems at home?" Dani tries. "With school? With Udo?" Each of these guesses elicits no different reaction. "With your friends?"

Here she stops shaking her head, sniffs, blows her nose.

"Is that it? Is it social?"

Yoon-jee lifts her head up. "What is . . ."

"With friends?"

Her gaze falls back to the floor. "I can't . . ."

"You can, Yoon-jee. You can trust me."

The girl's bloodshot eyes are ancient and delphic. "Promise they won't find out I tell."

The counselors are cautioned against making promises to students, especially in regard to confidentiality. She looks away. "Yoon-jee, you need to describe the situation so I can try to help."

But it isn't until Dani looks back at the girl and nods that she spills it: "A girl's dad is in Jopok and will kill my parents if I wear clouds."

Although Dani understands all but one of the words, the whole sentence seems foreign.

"What is Jopok, Yoon-jee?"

"Is like . . . is like . . . Korean Italians. Korean Italian gang . . ."

"The Korean mafia?"

Yoon-jee nods.

"And your friend's dad's is in the Jopok and will hurt your family if . . ."

"Will kill, yes."

"If you do what?"

"If I don't do everything my friend says."

"What kind of stuff does she ask you to do?"

"Do all her homework plus all mine, stay up talking to her all night, wake her up for class every morning . . ."

"What about the clouds?"

Again Yoon-jee's gaze falls to the carpet. "Today I wear new shirt with clouds, and I don't know she was only girl who can wear clouds."

"Are you talking about Min-ah?"

Yoon-jee's head shoots back up. "She can't know I tell."

"Well, you didn't really tell me her name, right?" Dani says. "All you mentioned were clouds. I'm just a good guesser."

Yoon-jee lets slip a smile.

"How are things going with Udo?" Dani asks, referring to the unlikely friendship between Yoon-jee and a freshman boy from Austria who speaks as little English as she—possibly the most adorable couple Dani has ever encountered.

The smile wins, and Dani envisions cartoon hearts popping above Yoon-jee's head. "He's so cute."

V.

When Dani told her about the conversation, Cora Csoke, the residence life manager, knew she would have to get the dean involved. Janelle Bazelguette thanked her for her prompt attention to the matter and set up a nine o'clock meeting for Monday morning.

Relaying the news of ad hoc meetings always proves distasteful, this time doubly so.

Dani looked anxious. "Can we be sure that Yoon-jee's name won't be brought up?"

"We'll try to keep it anonymous, the whole 'multiple source' route probably."

"If Min-ah finds out who told us, I'm sure she'll take it out on Yoon-jee."

"Then she'll get sent home," Cora shrugged. "We're not gonna put up with this bullshit."

Informed at sign-in Sunday night, Min-ah met the news with a momentary scowl. Her hair was cut at a sharp upward angle at her shoulders, ending in tips like the ears of a lynx. She wore her powder-blue cloud jacket as usual, the one with the multicolored zipper teeth that traveled all the way up and around the baggy hood. Min-ah quickly traded her annoyance for exaggerated bafflement.

"What is the meeting about?"

"No worries," Cora assured her. "We just want to talk over a few things, some rumors that've been going around."

"What rumors?"

"We'll talk about it tomorrow."

"Who has been talking about me?"

"Nine o'clock, Min-ah. You know where Janelle's office is?"

"Nine o'clock . . . so early."

From Yoon-jee, she expected panic. Instead, sorrow. The detachment of having set into motion a series of actions big enough as to turn her into a spectator of her own life. Her words were urgent but her voice was resigned.

"But . . . I said she could not find out. Dani promised."

"Don't worry, Yoon-jee—you won't be at the meeting. Janelle is really good at conflict resolution. We'll make sure to leave you out of it."

"It won't matter . . ."

"You said Min-ah picks on all the freshmen and sophomores, right?"

"I am very youngest."

"It could be any one of you who came to us. Or several of you," Cora said. "It'll be very clear to her that, if it continues, there'll be big consequences. Like she could get sent home. So you'll have to come tell us if she says anything more. Understand?"

"But what about my family?"

"Min-ah was making that up to try and scare you. Her family's not in the Korean mafia."

"How do you know? They can afford Andermatt."

"We have to try, Yoon-jee. We can't let this keep happening."

"You will only make it worse."

Monday morning Cora arrives a few minutes late, already finding Dani and Min-ah assembled in the small lobby outside Janelle's office. "Good morning," she says but receives no reply. "Is Janelle in?"

"She's on the phone," Dani responds. "She said she'd just be a minute."

Sitting, Cora attempts to meet Min-ah's glare with a smile devoid of syrup or sympathy or smirk. A completely commonplace smile. "How are you this morning, Min-ah?"

"Dani said this is about a complaint."

The residence life director almost glances over at her counselor. That wasn't really the right way to have put it.

"Who has complained about me?"

"Multiple sources have come to us expressing concern over a particular issue."

"Many people are complaining about me?"

"Just wait. We'll all be able to talk about it in just a minute."

Min-ah settles back into her chair, glowering. Notes and cartoons and checkerboard designs cover her thin wrists up to where they disappear inside her sleeves. She catches Cora looking and puts her hands in the pockets of her cloud jacket.

As soon as the door opens and Janelle appears, Min-ah quickly stands and smiles, giving a little giggle when the dean welcomes them into her office. Janelle is dressed today in a pantsuit and leather clogs, a diaphanous scarf in full bloom around her shoulders. Books and labeled binders line the particleboard desk along the back wall. Janelle quickly turns off the computer monitor that affords a brief glimpse of an inbox deluged with messages. Several lamps cast a calming tungsten glow on the four chairs that face each other over a round coffee table.

"Please sit down."

"Thank you," Min-ah beams, and Cora can already tell that she's slipped into the thicker accent and more limited fluency behind which international students sometimes hide.

For a minute or two, Janelle puts on a show of being flustered, saying, "Sometimes this place is *just madness,*" but smiling in the practiced way that enlists Cora, Dani, and the student as co-combatants against the madness—rather than its sources. She offers banana bread, disclosing a few tidbits about her weekend.

Dani and Cora decline the foil-wrapped loaf, but Min-ah daintily plucks a small piece and pops it into her mouth, saying, "Mmmm, so good!"

Then the clumsy moment when conversation must segue into business. "Min-ah," Janelle leans forward, "it has come to our attention that some of the upper-school Korean girls are acting

toward the younger girls in an antagonistic way . . . Do you understand that word?"

Min-ah shakes her head in feigned apology.

"That's okay. What we've heard is that some of the older girls
are acting like bullies, bossing the first- and second-year students
around. We called together this little meeting in hopes that you
can help us understand what's going on."

Min-ah casts her eyes downward.

"Does the way I describe the situation sound accurate?"

Min-ah nods. "Some girls, yes. Is like back home, except
no moms."

"Thank you for your honesty, Min-ah. But what you need to
understand is that this isn't back home, and that behavior can't
be tolerated in a school setting."

"What is . . ." Min-ah trails off, playing with her zipper.

"It has to stop. If it keeps happening, we might need to have
a more serious meeting and think about sending people home."

"But . . . but . . . it's not me!" the girl pleads earnestly, now
looking the dean in the eyes.

"That's not the information that has come to us—"

"From who? Who is saying these things?"

"That's not what's important, Min-ah. You're the oldest
Korean girl at the school. I know this gives you a lot of clout, a lot
of power and influence over the others. Do you know what I mean
when I say 'pecking order?'"

"Pecking?"

Janelle decides that this one isn't worth the time trying to
explain. "Unfortunately, this type of thing has happened in previous years—"

"When I was freshman, four years ago," Min-ah interrupts,

"the older girls, they would make me cut my arms and help them throw up, and they would say every day that I am fat and I must throw up also." Tears. "I promised that when I am senior I will not do such things. But the other girls . . . I do not have this power. It is not pecking order. I don't know why freshman girl would say my name. I'm the least who does this."

She accepts a tissue from Janelle and dabs at her eyes. Cora suspects she wore extra mascara today.

"I'm sorry you had to go through all of that," Janelle says. "It makes me very sad to hear that those kinds of things occur at this school. We're not trying to make accusations—and if what you're saying is true, I'm sorry about what we're putting you through."

"How come Jill is not here?" Min-ah asks. "She is my counselor."

"Today is Jill's day off, and Dani was kind enough to sit in for her."

"The girl is on Dani's hall?"

"I was hoping I could ask for your help in making our campus more peaceful for everyone," Janelle continues.

Min-ah nods.

"I think you have more power among the Korean girls than you're telling us, especially in the art department. And I think you know this. I want to ask you to use that power to help these younger students who are feeling so threatened."

Min-ah opens her eyes wide, her lips quivering. "Can you not tell me who is suffering?"

Now Janelle looks away, affected. Now down at the floor for a moment before turning again to the student.

"As I said before, Min-ah, that's not the point of this meeting. I need you to set a good example for the other seniors and to stand up for the younger students if they're being treated badly. And I want you to tell us if anything irresponsible is going on—Jill or Cora or me."

"Tell Dani?" Min-ah asks.

"Yes, you can tell any of the staff. That would be hugely helpful. Can you do that for us?"

"Yes, I want to help," she smiles. "The girls do pick on Yoon-jee."

IV.

Your daughter called again today.

Uh-oh. Same complaints?

What else? The older girls are being mean, saying things about her in class in Korean so the teachers don't understand.

Do no adults speak Korean?

I guess not.

What did you tell her?

That she must toughen up and respect the older girls.

What if they *are* being cruel to her?

She said she's afraid for us because one of the girl's friends is in the Jopok, that she has threatened to have them hurt us and Tzu-ping.

Yoon-jee has a large imagination.

She says she wants to come home, that she must.

What? I should talk to her.

I think it is better to not react to such talk. I reminded her that this is her dream but the sacrifice of us all. I made her repeat after me, *I am a lucky girl.*

She is lucky. One day she will realize, when she is older and commands the respect.

The adults will call us, I am sure, if it gets very bad.

III.

Blake Sikorski was the only counselor who openly admitted to liking the Thursday administrative meetings: the confidentiality, the access to higher-ups, the flirtation with outright gossip, the scoop. An ironic, distanced enjoyment, he tried to assure himself. But sometimes he wondered . . .

Shit-stompin' boots were a necessary component of his Thursday uniform, as was a tucked-in cowboy shirt (the letter but not the spirit of business casual). In the basement of the administrative building he would buy a fifty-cent cup of shitty coffee from one of those machines from the seventies that had somehow escaped retirement, feigning a shot of whiskey, passing a hand over his eyes (a phrase in writing he'd only recently come to understand), invoking a movie line from some champion of world-weariness: Clive Owen or Harrison Ford or—the world-weariest in the world—Tommy Lee Jones.

Wallowing in the intolerability—that's how he survives here, modeling himself a voice of reason but not the asshole kind. He had run into some trouble two months into the job when a parent screamed at him on the phone, extinguishing any confidence he'd been stoking. His own father had given him some strange advice, words that had buoyed him thus far.

"You're having a rough time because you're trying to love your job," he said during one late-night phone call. "Almost nobody loves their job."

"So I should just . . . be okay with hating it?"

"No, hatred leads to misery and unemployment. I'm talking about indifference. You have to fashion yourself a bastion of imperviousness if you want to do a good job and survive that snake pit."

His father never talked like this. Never spoke of love or hate or snake pits. "Won't indifference make people think I don't care?"

"Not indifference to the *tasks*," his father stressed. "To the *people*."

"Are you sure that's not horrible advice?"

"If you befriend a student, he'll get expelled. If you hate a student he'll use that against you, and you'll be right back where you are now. Invulnerability—place that word foremost in your mind. Cover your ass."

And it had worked. He'd found heart in his heartlessness, comfort in his ability to handle the most awkward residential conflicts. He told his father it didn't seem like any way to live. Would he do permanent harm to his humanity? It's only a year, his father had consoled him, only nine months. Only seven more.

But now it's five months, and as he walks into the sterile, windowless conference room, he wonders if this is what a calling sounds like. He takes a scalding sip and selects the quote he'll repeat to himself throughout the day: "I like nightmares."

He talks too much at these meetings, is fully aware of his infamy. But amidst all the bumbling and uncertainty and evasion, he relishes the clearly spoken fact, the opinion backed by solid incident, the connection cautiously suggested. Solution and recognized follow-through. His favorite: a contribution or anecdote regarding a student he shouldn't necessarily know, but does—a boy who lives in another building, or a shy girl—the rolled eyes and impatience at his unnecessary stretching of this torturous meeting past the allotted hour.

Today he hopes to dominate a solid minute rehashing his most recent phone call to Mr. Solorio, the father who had earlier berated Blake and seems now to broodingly despise him even more for his virtuosic composure and dispassion. But, as the meeting progresses, the conversation is stalled around the particulars of a disagreement involving several Korean students, and Blake finds himself with little to contribute.

"Next up, Min-ah Meng"—Janelle coaxes the room down the list of students—"purportedly one of the main antagonists in this group of seniors. I met with her on Monday along with Cora and Dani, and I think we had a really good conversation. Although she didn't take complete ownership, she opened up quite a bit, and I'm confident that we've enlisted her help in defusing this potentially volatile situation. What have you all noticed in the dorms?"

"I'm less optimistic about how the meeting went," Dani speaks up from the seat right next to Blake. Her voice wavering and scratchy, her eyes tired, her notes disorganized—she reminds Blake of himself three months ago.

Sometimes he zones out and, instead of listening to his coworkers, just watches the glowing spreadsheet projected on the wall, where Marilyn, the school therapist, records minutes for each student:

Dani: Min-ah acting outwardly kind toward Yoon-jee, but suspicions that she's instructing other Korean students to torment her for "narking." Spread mean rumore about Yoon-jee to Udo, Yoon-jees interest. Udo now avoiding Yoon-jee. JB: wonders if other students will varify. Call to parents? Yoon-jee to meet with Marilyn?

"I'm not sure we can trust everything Yoon-jee is saying," Bo LaMott wants everyone to know. "Cindy says she's really been flaking out in class lately. Apparently just the other day she was tracing a diamond shape in the back of her hand with an eraser, over and over. Went through the skin."

"I should definitely talk with her," Marilyn reaffirms softly, writing a note in her lime-green, leather-bound planner.

"And her artwork has a pretty morbid side to it. The other day Cindy had them do a sketch of their non-dominant hand; hers was pretty good, but she'd drawn a string around the pinkie finger, and the string was drawn on so tight that the tip of the finger had shriveled up from lack of blood. Min-ah, on the other hand, never really causes us any problems, except that she's doing the tattoo thing too, which, as I've said, is a known gateway—"

"For anyone who doesn't know," Janelle explains, "something similar to this happens most every year, this Korean girl . . . situation. There's this vicious queen-bee mentality where the oldest seniors boss around the younger girls, ridicule them in their own language, and we can never really figure out who's doing what and who's making stuff up. It's not just here either—lots of boarding schools with significant Korean populations express comparable frustrations. But nobody's ever really proposed a good solution. Somebody could make a lot of money writing a decent book on the subject."

"Have we thought of hiring an ESL teacher who speaks Korean?" Blake volunteers. He sees Dani flash him a thankful "Ya *think*?"

"Yeah, maybe we just need a bigger queen bee," someone jokes.

"So how's the somnolent, soporific songwriting career?" Blake asks Dani.

The meeting is over and all the counselors are heading toward the cafeteria.

"Oh, alright. This really great melody came to me the other night, but I haven't been able to figure it out. I think it's gone."

"I'm sorry for your loss."

As they step from the concourse into the chill glare of sunlight on ice, she asks, "So how are the Korean boys? Do you have any on your hallway?"

"Three. They're totally chill."

"I guess they'd have to be to put up with their women."

Blake lets it be known this is his type of joke. "Actually I had this really surreal cultural moment last Saturday night. Won-shik came to me while I was at the desk—it was twelve thirty a.m.—and he tells me that Jin-ho's feeling really sick. I, of course, say let me see the kid. Won-shik holds up his hands, says that's not how we do it. 'He sends me to tell you how he's doing.' Over the next hour, Won-shik updated me three or four times on Jin-ho's status, always urging me not to go check up on him. I got the impression he wasn't dangerously sick, and I didn't smell anything suspicious—not from these guys. So I just recommended he go to Health Services in the morning. Won-shik agrees and says that *I* will need to accompany him—Jin-ho, that is. Once I figured out he was serious, I was like are you fuckin' kidding me? Do I really have to get up at eight a.m.? It's a five-minute walk—can't he make it by himself? Then, very solemnly, Won-shik says, 'In our culture someone always takes care of us when we're sick.' And then I understood this was something I wasn't going to understand. He was, I guess, relinquishing his best friend's care to me . . . and that got me out of bed on my day off."

"Trade you your Koreans for mine."

They step into the cafeteria, into clanking silverware, student chatter, and the reek of mass food preparation.

Five minutes later, seated by the wide wall of windows with a table full of counselors, their plates mutually mounded with chicken vindaloo, chickpea shawarma, and naan bread, the cafeteria's attempt at the "Taste of India," Dani says to Blake, "I appreciated your suggestion about hiring an ESL teacher who speaks Korean."

"I appreciated how that conversation unfolded: big problem . . . happens every year . . . any suggestions? . . . no? . . . let's move on. I like nightmares."

"I've started trying to learn the language, and as much about their culture as I can, just the past few days."

Blake gulps pop. "You better hurry."

"What does that mean?"

"It means you can't save them all."

"I feel so powerless, so—"

"Dani, as a wise man once said, successfully hating your job is better than trying and failing to love it."

"But you love this job . . . right?"

Blake takes a big bite of chicken and leans back in his chair, grinning, chewing with his mouth open. "Let me give you some advice . . ."

"Are you sure that's not terrible advice?" she says when he finishes. She's at a time in her professional career when she doesn't trust anyone who seems confident in themselves.

Blake shrugs. "Just giving you a rare opportunity to learn without learning."

II.

Cindy Brandemihl had decided to resign at the end of the year, but she was nervous to inform Bo. Part of her knew she should be

thankful to have landed such a secure job, and she'd made her decision without confirming a position elsewhere. True, she had a few
interviews in the spring, but part of her honestly hoped that the
end of the year would find her floating. Although she'd secured an
optimistic dealer for the jewelry she designed, she had zero expec-
tations of making it as an artist. She might as well write poetry.

But it was days like this one that had lately convinced her that
she was officially living for other people—for her students and their
parents and the school administration, not for herself and all that
stuff it says on her artist statement. She'd only taught for four hours
today, but they were spread out enough that it felt like an eight-
hour day, and those segments of time between classes never yielded
the productivity they had back in grad school. Then three hours
setting up for and attending a visiting artist's exhibition none of
the students would have gone to if it wasn't mandatory. An hour
checking email and succumbing to internet distractions, and now
it's nine o'clock and she still has a giant pile of student sketchbooks
to grade before making a closed circuit of herself and Netflix. Then
maybe seven hours of sleep, then another similar day.

She dislikes that whole "Those who can't do, teach" maxim,
but sometimes it seems as if, for her purposes, she might as well
be dead—even when she can fight for a little studio time. And so
her most daring daydreams include her *not* finding another job in
academia, working as a waitress like she had in grad school, or at
a greenhouse maybe. "Is this really what you want to be doing in
twenty years?" some wizened veteran will ask her, and she will
reply, "This isn't what I want to be doing *today*." But it will be,
because two years of hectic comfort have taught her that a job that
builds toward nothing is preferable to a job that builds toward a
future you don't want.

A gap in employment? Absolutely.

She opens the first sketchbook—a sort of visual journal she assigns her drawing students—to find that it had obviously been rushed through the day of. Interesting concept though, various marker drawings of places where hearts traditionally appear (Valentine's cards, candy boxes, enclosing initials, the end of Cupid's arrows, etc.), the cartoon hearts replaced by anatomical ones, with tubes and spurts and sheen. She openly laughs at the protagonist of the board game Operation pleading "Quit playing games with my heart" as his is tweezed and his nose lights up in alarm. Good enough. A-minus for Udo.

The next one, Yoon-jee's, is so meticulously rendered that, although she can't help but give her an A, it doesn't really resemble a spontaneous font of inspiration and nascent ideas so much as a series of planned, well-executed drawings.

The first few depict a very fat, laughing Southeast Asian woman hanging out with hens in various social situations: having coffee, watching *Dr. Phil*, playing Scrabble, shopping. Then one single drawing of a man in his organized suburban garage, surrounded by large cardboard boxes branded in black magic marker with the words FAMILY, RELIGION, and WORK. Again, a shit-eating grin as he beams at the viewer and tapes up a final box labeled DEATH. A little heavy-handed. But cute how the tape is a tiny strip of real duct tape.

The last series is of exit signs stenciled with various synonyms: EGRESS, OUTLET, GONE, EXODUS, ESCAPE, LEAVE, etc. Below each is a drawing of a black-haired girl looking downward, her face concealed by bangs. Every turn of the page shows a different perspective of her, like she's rotating in a circle, always wearing the same blank zippered jacket. And between her and the signs, a connecting line grows thicker and more detailed with each page turned. A flipbook of sorts, but Cindy resists treating it as such.

After maybe twenty drawings, she begins to turn the pages more quickly, impatient for some kind of variety. She stops. The line connecting the exit sign to the girl twists into a rope and snakes around her neck. A noose. She wasn't looking down. The sign reads WAY OUT. Her hand shaking, Cindy turns the page, everything the same except that the sign reads SOON, and the hanged girl's jacket is colored-in: powder blue with clouds.

Digging her phone from her pocket, she turns another page and actually recoils from the book. Yoon-jee had worn through the rest of the pages and the back cover writing I AM A LUCKY GIRL on top of itself again and again and again.

"Hi, Bo," Cindy says when he picks up. "Sorry to call so late."

I.

Dani has made compilation CDs, then playlists, for every school year's favorite songs ever since seventh grade. Summer slips by uncatalogued. Like a particular smell, the chosen songs evoke the moods and atmospheres of that year more perfectly than any photograph or journal entry could. Though she values the existence of the mixes, she doesn't listen to them that often. It seems the nature of rock 'n' roll to attach itself to transitory visions, shameful stages, and drama too ugly to want to relive.

Over the past week, she's been listening to the Zombies' *Odessey and Oracle* incessantly, to the point that she risks soon coming to despise it. In particular, tonight, "Hung Up on a Dream" has been tumbling all over itself in her head. Her brain's DJ keeps skipping ahead to the next verse, creating a frantic canon remix. She doesn't mind this simple song claiming a coveted three and a half minutes on this year's playlist, but what she fears is that it has become so inextricably linked to tonight's pain that, once the immediacy dulls, the melancholic surrender she attaches to the song will make her never want to hear it again. Solace provided is a beautiful gift, the need for it pathetic.

She'd turned her music to a fully audible level before retreating to bed. She needed familiarity, and she knew there'd be no writing new riffs tonight. During Dani's closing desk shift, Janelle had showed up—usually a bad sign, certainly at eleven p.m., a fact very obvious to every student in the lobby as well. Dani could immediately see the speculation start to fly.

Taking her into the back office, Janelle explained that they would need to see Yoon-jee tonight. The dean wore a Harvard sweatshirt and jeans. Dani had never seen her without makeup on.

"Tonight?"

"Yes. She turned in some work to Cindy Brandemihl that makes us concerned about self-harm, or possibly against a fellow student. Marilyn is on her way."

"Yeah, I was hoping to talk to you soon about Yoon-jee's situation," Dani said, though Janelle's eyes were already heading out the office door, up the stairs, and down the freshman hallway. "I'm not sure if we've done everything we can, or if we're going about it in the right way. I think maybe we need to have a meeting with just—"

When they knocked on Yoon-jee's door and entered, she didn't seem surprised to see the dean of students and the school therapist at such a late hour. On her bed, an open suitcase.

Her roommate, Claudia, however, did look surprised. Frantic. "What's she *talking* about?"

Back in the office, Janelle and Marilyn suggested that surely

Yoon-jee didn't mean those things. They could get her professional help in town.

Dani had never seen a student so relaxed and comfortable in the face of such serious consequences. Yoon-jee would allow the adults to speak for a minute or two, then would reply with some variation on "I will hurt her. If you keep me here, it's my promise."

Maybe she'd actually read the student handbook. Either way, she'd discovered a startlingly simple way that a student could bring about immediate change.

As the administration tried to muster its resources, Dani was left alone in the office with her student.

"I'm sorry." Dani felt like she was defending herself. "I'm learning Korean."

Yoon-jee understood. "I'm learning American."

Yoon-jee was taken to Health Services on twenty-four-hour watch, and Janelle called her parents to arrange travel. It was nearly three p.m. tomorrow in South Korea, luckily.

Subs so fast you'll freak

At that moment you knew. Not yet hungry, but about to be hungry. Not yet wailing, but about to freak out. Then cradled, kissed, cooed to—and you were nursing. Despite your initial misgivings, despite the things that still surprised you, this place was suitable. A place where needs would be met before you even knew of their existence.

The gap between more and enough never closes. Was it really that they prepared the sandwich for you so quickly? True, it was in your hand before the words were out of your mouth. But we're all looking for an excuse.

To love like no one's watching. To dance like you don't need the money. Work like you've never been hurt.

You have questions
we have answers

If puppies are my favorite thing—which they are—how come I turn away in disgust when one rolls around on its back? Radio store, how exactly is cuteness affecting evolution these days? And how many of the teams can you name from Legends of the Hidden Temple? *If flashbacks exonerated Andy Dufresne in* The Shawshank Redemption, *why are we still investigating Russian interference in the 2016 election? Tell me, why did Jean Sibelius stop writing music in the last thirty years of his life? How do you pronounce Järvenpää, and why? Is knowing the difference between stalactites and stalagmites ever going to come in handy? Why don't I just shut the fuck up? If you flattened the world's landmasses so they were one inch above sea level, how much of the planet's surface area would land cover? Are Doc Martens uncool enough again that I can buy a pair? Where did you get that Marvin the Martian leather jacket? What would possess a person to make a movie that's not about dinosaurs? How could we have known Roseanne would say something off-color on color? If nobody's onstage, who's making those noises? If global warming is real, how come I'm not currently drowning? Which last of species will be the last of species?*

What, an adventure? Where do I go for help? What do I think about that? I'm off to bury my various boners in ice. Primates of the future, please: Anthropocene Park.

When you're here you're family

"I'M not the one who's hungry. You're the hungry people." The hostess is upset. "You're the ones who want a breadstick passing down your gullets forever. Seat yourselves!" The hostess stomps off, slamming behind her the door of what appears to be a supply closet. "Shit . . . shit . . . shit . . . ," one of my fellow patrons is appraising my recent oil paintings, which are hanging on every wall of the Olive Garden. "Now that I like," he says of an embarrassing colored-pencil self-portrait I did in high school. He awards it a blue ribbon. The menopausal waitress interrupts me in the middle of my drink order to dash outside and do calisthenics, each breath venting her hot flashes into the December night. The chef sits at the bar, carefully arranging precarious stacks of mail at perfect right angles and voting for demagogues. "Sit down for two seconds and eat something, would ya?" I invite the waitress, but she's still chewing her first bite of salad when she dashes off again to bring me my alfredo dipping sauce and to clean up after a blue cat that keeps eating plant leaves then vomiting them onto the carpet. "Shit . . . shit . . . shit . . ." The chef begins feeding one stack of mail into a paper shredder, yells at the hostess to turn down her goddam music. "She's beautiful," some old woman says, clasping my shoulder with a liver-spotted claw.

"Just remember—there's only twelve eggs in a carton."
The waitress appears by my side with the Parmesan
shredder: "Tell me when—" "When," I cut her off. "Tell
me when," she repeats, and keeps turning the crank.
The gagging cat is approaching my shoes, and soon I
will have to take some kind of action. "Shit . . . shit . . . ,"
the stranger keeps appraising my art. "Now that, that
I like."

The Unquestionable Sincerity
of Fire Alarms

Sam

But, all of it, ruined. By Corey Little. Who *is* little. Whose eyes look permanently blackened, like a raccoon's, and whose skin is so pale his veins show through purple. Who'd spent the whole drive sitting there without a Discman or Game Gear or anything. Just staring out the window. Ruining everything.

Sure enough, when Sam's mom finally wrangles the key card away from her husband and grants them entrance into room 212 of the Wausau AmericInn, two queen-size beds grin up at the husband and wife and the two thirteen-year-old boys who aren't related and don't much like each other. Sam Hackbarth wondering how he can shame Corey into saying he *wants* to sleep on that chair in the corner.

"Which bed do you guys want?"

Fuck you, fuck you, fuck you, fuck you, he directs at his mom—not because the situation is really her fault, but because of how she's trying to shrug it off as no big deal. An attempt to save money, his dad had claimed. But there was a tender threat in his voice not to ask more.

Guys used to have to sleep together all the time, Sam tries to tell himself, conjuring up a frontier scenario where a family of twelve shared a one-room cabin. But he can't reassure-away the idea that, for the rest of his life, any time he sees Little, there will be an unspoken bond between them: me and you, that one weekend. The worst player on the team.

Sam grabs his skateboard and leaves the room. Part of him enjoys the idea of abandoning Corey to his parents so they can work out the sordid details of their unnatural cohabitation without him. Maybe he'll come back and the two beds will be pushed together. He imagines the three of them sitting there in bathrobes, eating peanut butter crackers.

Liam

Liam Ihrke collects followers as he walks down a hallway lit sluttily by faux-gold sconces. Outside it's dreary and overcast, but still bright by comparison—and warm, the kind of weather that gets you expecting spring even though it's February. The air smells salty, as if they're near a coast instead of in the flat middle of a large continent. The asphalt is new, dark and puddled with snowmelt. They skate their way around the AmericInn, the parked cars thinning out as they approach the ass end of the building. A field hatched by snowmobile tracks, the highway off-ramp. A few of them try and mostly fail to do tricks, then have to catch up with the group.

Behind a dumpster bounded by a plastic picket fence, they come across a group of teammates dripping Visine in their eyes.

"You just missed it." Nick Spezak, the goalie, throws a lazy punch at Liam's gut. "Got our fog on."

It's a sort of joke. Liam had made an honest effort to like weed for a while.

"King, Cootchie," Nick nods at two of the new arrivals, both of whom have unfortunate nicknames. He throws a V over his nipple for Alan Roo, who'd once famously thought cootchies meant boobs (which made the phrase "cootchie cutters" somewhat of a mystery).

And poor Austin Gimberlin—you'd think a guy wouldn't mind the nickname King Cock, the Burger King crown and coronation ceremony the parents had watched with confusion. But it isn't *his* cock. Soon after a few brave pioneers had started showering after practices, he'd commented that Grant Lodermeier had the biggest one on the team. It was supposed to sound offhanded.

"Party in my room tonight."

"When?"

"Quarter after my mom's second Zima."

"Will there be booze?"

"However much my dad can lose track of."

"Girls?"

"Desk clerk told me there's a volleyball team staying here." Nick looks back at the AmericInn. "Alan, maybe you can get them to help you out. Free cootchie informational meeting, room 219."

"Cootchies: identification and classification."

"Cootchie Q&A."

"Cootchie cutters: unknown risks."

"Caring for your cootchies."

Eventually it stops.

"Did you see the other teams?" Austin speaks up, choosing his words with painful care. "Sun Prairie's on the first floor. They're all wearing these CCM tracksuits."

"How were their cocks?" Nick asks. "Did they let you measure them?"

Liam notices: Austin's not the only one blushing. Nick's blushing too. He's jealous. Liam laughs and everyone joins in because they think he's laughing at King. Add some woundedness to Austin's humiliation, since Liam's usually the one sticking up for the losers.

Some of the guys take to the lot to work on their kickflips and ollies. Liam leans against the dumpster's fence and just watches. He's the only one on the team who's actually good at skateboarding, but he's been doing it less and less. Even though his nonparticipation is building his mystique as a distanced judge of everyone else's bumbling, the real reason is because he's on his way out. In a year's time he'll be wearing clothes that fit and getting good grades. The Freshjive shirt he'd saved up to buy at the Station, his baggy brown cargo pants, his black Sal 23 Etnies—it feels more and more like just another type of uniform. He can't watch his friends bust their asses without hearing circus music.

He knows the same thing might happen with hockey some day.

Jay

"Go Sam!"

"That's not Sam," Jay tells his wife.

She squints and leans forward three inches to better identify the swarming blue jerseys on the ice below.

"It's Corey Little." Jay glances at Sam's parents, but he's not sure if they heard. Nobody wants their son confused with Corey Little. "The kid whose mom . . ."

"Oh. I can't keep half these kids straight."

"You don't need to. Neither can their parents."

Sometimes he thinks it's wrong, how charmed he is by his wife's general sense of bewilderment. A belittlement, he worries, the part of you that lunges out at such moments. According to all metrics that might be used to measure intelligence—education level, occupation, Trivial Pursuit—she's smarter than him. But that doesn't keep her from looking mystified when he reminds her that banks are closed on Sundays, or that it's not "all intensive purposes." These moments reveal a lack of complete accessibility that, in his experience, is more exciting than any nirvanic merging of identities. Off in her own world, leaving something still to pursue after seventeen years of marriage.

"That one's ours." Jay points as Austin picks up the puck and stickhandles out of the zone.

"I know that."

See? Every other woman on earth would have just scowled or swatted him. For Gwen, there had still been just a flicker of doubt.

Would she even remember Rice Lake last year, when they'd rented an unnecessary hotel room just to escape from the boy for an hour? They hadn't bothered to ask the other parents at the pool to keep an eye on him.

One way or another, he's made sure there's vacancies this weekend at the AmericInn. It's been a while since their last time together.

Because of their last time together.

In his pocket, his hand finds a tiny piece of paper, rolls and unrolls it like a scroll. Between games, the kids had decided on a strip-mall Chinese buffet despite Coach K's warning that all-you-can-eat MSG is not the best pregame fuel. They'd won the first game against Onalaska, giving the meal a festive air. But something was bothering Jay. Something about the disparity between Wausau and China, soft serve and General Tso, hockey hats and silk screens of waterfalls and dragons. Why are all the kids calling his son King, and why does his son hate it?

Two waitresses hovered around the tables, ready to whisk away plates if left unattended for half a second. The boys made a competition of eating as much as they could before their fullness announced itself, and Jay imagined the total consumption of the hockey team mounded like the piles of gray snow in the parking lot. Prone to a miserliness that's unsafe in buffet situations, Jay would normally have joined them—but the nerves in his stomach wouldn't allow it. As if he was the jittery athlete, back in his state championship days when any deviation from his routine would presage doom.

Their fullness, the sense that they'd made a mistake, hit the whole team all at once. They held their bellies and groaned, expressed total disinterest in the orange slices and fortune cookies that were to be the cadence of their dining experience.

Jay broke open a cookie, popped one of its folds into his mouth, planned on paying its message no more attention than usual.

The fuck—?

His wife stands as the entire rink gets its wind knocked out. All the parents are standing now, their faces aghast. Jay stands, looks down at the ice.

There, sprawled and motionless by the corner boards: that one's ours.

Corey Little

"Remember his number," Coach K tells the bench after Austin's helped off and the refs chewed out. Not you, Little, might as well've added.

But Corey thinks: me. Because it never would be. Eyes find Fifteen, imagine his skating body laid out on the ice. Enough size difference to require surprise.

A way back in, prove yourself to the team.

Windows where the far wall meets the ceiling, sun in your eyes if you catch the angle. Parallelogram of shiny wet where it turns the ice gold. Fifteen breaks out of the zone with the puck.

For a second: that minute begging Austin's legs to move. Imagine Fifteen motionless, head immobilized on a stretcher.

The sooner you pity, the sooner you're pitied.

Think of how shocked they'll be. *Corey LITTLE?*

He takes off, enough strides for charging, for a game misconduct—

Shit—crashes into the boards a stride behind Fifteen. Timed it wrong or chickened out or pitied. *Injured?* ref's eyes ask as well, whistle hand hesitating. No idea what to call since Corey didn't actually make contact.

He reassembles himself, limp-skates toward the bench. It's the same as a penalty kill till he can make the change. Hears cheering, cowbells, sees teammates hanging their heads—and Little doesn't need to look.

Sooner you pity—

Like Mom still thinks she gets to give advice.

The Parents

Oh no. Last night we *owned* the pool.

Why does it have to be Sun Prairie? The parents have commandeered the hot tub, all the tables, and in the deep end our sons' enemies are playing some variation on water polo that involves hitting each other with pool noodles. The boys must be mortified. Some open chairs on the periphery of the Sun Prairie zone, but the last thing I want to do is ask anything of them. Imagine the indignity. Yeah, Tony, thank you. I'll sit on the cooler. But get a beer first. There you go.

Are you kidding me? Did you really bring your goddam *cowbells* into the pool area? Even worse than pennies-in-a-milk-jug

Onalaska. Every goal, every penalty, every hit. Nothing's worse than losing to a cowbell team.

Ah, our counterparts in red and white: the messy alcoholics, the rich stiffs, the religious stiffs, the white trash, the white-collar criminals, the grandparent. Our token Asians are Sun Prairie's token blacks.

The next time he listens to that song, I'm turning it off. Does he know what that phrase means? Is it better if he does or if he doesn't? But then he'll no doubt pursue that type of thing more aggressively because Mom went out of her way to forbid it.

The fat one in the red Hockey Mom sweatshirt *has* to be number fifteen's mom. How can she wear that thing in the pool's hot chlorinated breath?

Sam isn't with the pool crowd. Probably out in the parking lot breaking his leg on that skateboard. Just get in the pool, boys. Waffling isn't going to make it any better. Don't look to your parents for a reminder of how one enters into the act of having fun.

Same cowbells we heard when number fifteen checked Austin from behind into the boards. Not even my son, but he was wearing blue and white, so for a half minute I tasted chaos. I'd have used my teeth to rend and tear. Austin's mom still in that feral state, upending a Seagram's without taking her eyes off Hockey Mom for a second.

When did it become every night? It's been . . . last Christmas, visiting my parents. The night we arrived, not a drop of alcohol anywhere in the house, and I thought: Show yourself you can do it. Exhausted from travel but mind racing, no fuzz to lull it sleepward, suddenly cognizant of the animal beside me snoring.

There you go. Jumping would have been better, but at least you've achieved wetness. Don't just stand there. Hurt one another.

Sam is furious about Corey staying with us, but what else could we have done? Tony's attitude isn't helping, using the situation to teach some hazy lesson about forbearance.

Filling out paperwork at the doctor, my mind rejected the most basic math, that drinking every night of the week doesn't mean seven drinks a week. There was that article, the oldest woman in the world attributing her longevity to Kentucky bourbon—but surely it will have repercussions. Poisoning myself a little every night.

Those murals are hideous, children and palm trees and jungle animals mutated by nuclear fallout. Kids every shade of skin color, pushing into green and pink.

Worst of all, the refs missed it. But at least the Sun Prairie fans gave Austin the cowbell treatment as he skated back to the bench—though it's tough to gauge the sincerity of a cowbell.

Sensitive bladder or not, did he have to use the bathroom while Corey was taking a shower? *I've gotta go. We're both men.* Not really. It's the first time I can recall not daring to make eye contact with my own son.

That's not the scary part, though. It's what the booze keeps me from thinking about.

A scream, some kid whose balls haven't dropped. Just Alan Roo—his teammates have given him the terrible nickname Cootchie—and the big disaster getting tagged in Marco Polo.

King Cock

"I found them," Austin tells Nick through the crack of space the chain allows the door to open.

Nick closes the door and opens it wide a second later.

"You should see their tracksuits," Austin grins.

"What is it with you and tracksuits?"

"It's halfway to pajamas."

For having such a crappy everything else, the AmericInn features a surprisingly spacious and well-equipped exercise room. And when Austin and Nick peer through the room's windows, it's full of tracksuits the color of sea foam.

"Those are nice," Nick admits.

"Told you."

"They've got their names sewn on them and everything. That lets us simultaneously check out their boobs while learning their names."

"Ladies, get ready for a *real* workout." Austin feels like a lion coiled to spring through the savannah grass.

"Easy there, King Cock. Stick to the plan."

Some of the Waunakee Lady Warriors are frozen into trembling yoga poses before a wall of mirrors, but most are draped over couches flipping through magazines and combing one another's hair. An impossible mirage, an island of mermaids offering succor to cabin boys lost at sea.

"I call the blonde, the one eating rice cakes. You get Celery Sticks."

"Why? Their friend's the hot one." Not that there's anything *wrong* with Celery Sticks.

"Exactly."

"If I give you the blonde, you have to promise to stop calling me King."

Nick turns to him with a look of sympathy. "You know I can't do that, buddy."

Sam

For a while, Sam had fun playing a new game they invented called Room Service. The rules: two players with hockey sticks slinging a tennis ball the length of a hallway, back and forth. Like Operation, you couldn't hit the edges. The chance that any door could open at any moment and admit a hapless intermediary added an element of suspense. Eventually they set up a triangular formation that covered two intersecting hallways. Then—when there were more people who wanted to participate than there were hallways—they designed a William Tell variation that involved humans as eyes-closed, crotch-covering obstacles. New bruises soon licked their bodies.

Finally, enough strangers interrupted the game that hotel staff was notified, and the boys scrambled up and down stairwells to avoid the night manager.

They reassembled back in the safety of Liam Ihrke's room, where commercials interrupted a mangled-for-TV *Under Siege* with greater and greater frequency as the action struggled to rise. When someone made the dozenth joke about King Cock, Liam said he'd told his brother the story—his brother, who plays for St. Lawrence—and his brother'd said, *Who cares? That's how guys talk in locker rooms. Your teammates are being little bitches.* That shut everyone up pretty quick. A game of Uno became one of those endless chores where everyone has thirty cards in their hands. When Sam folded everyone protested but was glad.

It isn't until he steps into room 212 and starts to reach for the light switch that he realizes his sleeping situation had become even gayer than he'd feared. He'd never thought to subtract his parents from the equation.

In what parking-lot light filters in through the curtains, he trips his way over the hockey equipment that litters the carpet.

Earlier, they'd dried everything with a hair dryer, filling the room with the odor of burnt Doritos.

It's like he's bypassing the totally empty bed and *choosing* to sleep with Corey. So fucking gay. There's something almost domestic about it, like they'd been sleeping together for years. He remembers Liam's brother and wonders, just for a moment, if instead of being gay he's been a little bitch all along.

He usually sleeps in just boxers, but tonight all he takes off are his shoes. Corey has every available blanket and cover pulled over him, and Sam inserts his body under just the top comforter. Frontier scenario, he reminds himself. A dozen burly dudes in one cabin. He tries to recall how dead tired he'd been during Uno, how he'd drawn card after card that were of no use to him. But all he can think of is the hockey equipment smell and how it's the smell of their mingled sweat. And how the mattress seems bowed toward the middle, a part of the conspiracy.

The Parents

It's back on my hands. There on the inside of the fourth finger where I first noticed it blooming a few summers ago. At the base of my right thumb. Don't let them see you contorting your nails to squeeze the blisters. But this one's ready to pop. They're almost invisible if you don't mess with them.

Do the other boys know yet? They wouldn't be playing with him in the pool like that. Or maybe they would—kids are more open-minded these days, even boys. But will they let him dress in the same locker room after they find out?

"Maybe I could get your advice on this. I've been thinking of putting together a shop in my basement, kind of like the one you have."

"Mine's not in my basement."

"You know what I mean. What are the essentials?"

"A mini fridge."

"Alan would probably get in there, make off with the booze."
No he wouldn't.

"That's the whole idea. Make sure the kids see what dudes do."

Why'd she go and do it? The only mom on the team with a
daughter Iris's age, the only one who knows how we leave them
behind, to their own devices, to learn from other figures of authority. Social authority. The only one I'd be friends with if I didn't
have to.

Why am I the one with the ambition? The only one who sees
how good he could be. He's not big, but that'll come. Sometimes
it's magic how that puck is just attached to his stick, one of those
paddles with the rubber balls, a yo-yo. He doesn't work hard, but
maybe he'll wake up, figure out this is the only time in his life he
can do these things, that so few kids get an opportunity like this.

"What brand do you go to? Bosch?"

"Shit, if you want to spend the most money, yeah. It's like I
told Nick when he said he wanted to play in net. I said fine, but I'm
not paying two grand so you look pretty. Get whatever's available,
Frankenstein style. Don't get too concerned that all your shit's the
same color." He spits into a Gatorade bottle.

"He played great today, by the way. Nick. He could have used
a . . . . *Little* help on that last goal."

"Why they put him out there with two minutes left I got no
fuckin' idea."

"But I guess we have to be nice to Corey for a while. It's gotta
be tough on him."

That's very good, how the wind sweeps through the room and

through the town square, how the foreground and background are bound together by one larger force. She's not squeezing your hand out of affection, you dummy, she just wants her hand back. That's one thing books can't do—I've never thought about it before—more than one thing happening at the same time. All this amorous talk blown together with manure and domestic service. Girl, *run*.

Why are you trying to impress that drunk piece of shit? Trying and failing to have those skills is worse than knowing you'll never need them. Go ahead and bite a chaw of tobaccy while you're at it, why don't you? Parade your kid reeking of pot and abuse.

I hate to leave her behind here at the end. Probably dropping those little unpinchable turds all over the house. That's okay, sweetie, you go wherever you want. God, I'd be okay if I came home and she was dead. I'd just cry for a few minutes. But the idea of . . .

I know what you want, and I'm fine with it happening. But how can you think about sex after what happened today, what those pieces of shit across the room cheered with their goddam cowbells? That's right, Hockey Mom, lean back and cackle. Give your cowbell the tiniest of tinkles.

"At first I thought, shit, *goalie*? Isn't that the most expensive position? Then I thought, at least it'll give me something to blame the bruises on." He laughs—whether because he's kidding or because he's not is impossible to tell.

"What's he up to tonight?"

"Has some fireworks we bought when we crossed the border. Just let me know when you smell smoke."

"I worry having the other teams staying in the same hotel with us. I hope they don't go headhunting."

"Boys will be shitheads."

Unlike fat finger. Dangling from my arm, the bloated hoof of a pig. Will it ever go back to how it was? I've never not healed before.

Maybe to pay for all this, equipment you can't patch fast enough, gas to get to games, the weekly tape tithe. Clear tape, cloth tape, friction tape. Where's her son, poor kid? Probably already asleep.

Alan cocked his head when I referred to us as the oldest parents on the team. They assume we're all in the same grade as well. Still getting used to socializing with couples twenty years younger than us. Does he ever think of how old we'll be when he graduates high school, college, when he starts a family? Does he ever think the phrase premenopause surprise? I guess his siblings can be the grandparent figures.

If it wasn't for Grant, he would be. Maybe Liam, too, but you can tell it's not going to last for him. That big nose and big forehead will turn troglodytic soon enough. It's the ones with those thin ankles you can tell are going to keep their beauty. Patrick got the best parts of both of us, for now.

Because he's a good man, he sat Darren down, told him that he loves hockey, but is it for sure an extracurricular he wants to take on? It wouldn't disappoint him. Because he's not a perfect man—because he's a man—he failed to ask if I was on board.

"I figure a miter saw is a good place to start."

"If you don't mind buying kraut, you've gotta go with the Bosch B3195. Chop and slide action like a hot knife through butter. Solid detents. Cam-action clamp and extension table come standard. Adjustable kerf plates to reduce tearout."

The Sun Prairie parents send up another swell of cowbells, as if they too are fans of the Bosch B3—whatever. For all I know I'm being fucked with.

"Or I got an old DeWalt I can sell you, eats into its own goddam frame when you use it compound."

This, I can tell, is an undesirable feature in a miter saw.

Are his eyes moving over their bodies right now, lingering on any one of his teammates? No, stop it. Part of being the confidante is not subjecting him to further suspicion. I wish he would go ahead and tell Andre. Andre won't care. What I have to keep telling myself.

What do animals in the wild do, just suffer on and on and on? What did humans do—for all but the sliver of history since the invention of painkillers, hospital wings they secretly call elephant graveyards. Would be a good name for a bar league team, Elephant Graveyard.

And this woman is the opposite of Emma Bovary, a happy breeder, auctioned off with the cattle. Faster and faster the oscillations, until Catherine Leroux halts it with her tar pit of a paragraph, her stupid . . . oh, what's the word? There it is! *Placidity*. What's it called when the one thing stands for the whole?

Is it how they show it on television? Those drab clothes with cheap elastic, soap that doesn't foam, gangs you have to pledge like some horror sorority? Ramen from the commissary a treat. Or is that just men's prisons? Maybe it's more like a retirement home you can't leave. What does she *do* all day? Am I horrible for thinking it sounds okay, not needing to take care of other people for a while, to focus just on keeping yourself alive.

Fine, it's fine, but don't ask me to shift one primal response into another. I'm still in the mood to kill. You shouldn't want to be around. Imagine the sweatshirted cowbelle painted on the wall, an amorphous caricature, shoveling terrified children into her guffawing maw.

"Are the Screwheads putting together a summer team this year?"

"We always say we're gonna take a summer off, but we always cave right before the deadline."

"Yeah, I don't think the Glue Crew is gonna have enough guys to fill."

"You guys are in . . . what, the Never-Ever League?"

"No, we're in the C League."

"I wish I could say we have spot for you—"

"I understand. You guys always have a full bench."

"What I mean is that we're trying to get some younger blood on the team. Seems like just a season or two ago *we* were the young guys."

If it wasn't for me talking to Coach K, he'd still be out there on Little's line. The whole team is Littles, though. I need to get him to the Capitols, or Pettit Selects. Remember what Coach Sabel said: *Call me as soon as he's five-ten, if that's before high school.* And laughed. One day the camera will find me in the crowd, pretending to pray, and it'll say Liam Ihrke's mom, and everyone watching will know the real reason he made it to the big show.

And this whole infrastructure of girls' sports just so these men can pretend it's fair. And boys. When's the last time Kurt went to one of Iris's games? Does he even know what sport she shrugged off this year? I guess it's good exercise either way.

It could be worse. You could be married to anyone else in this room.

There's no such thing as juniority, honey.

When's the last time I went swimming?

One more time. Ring those cowbells one more time.

"For sure."

What if this whole book is just about money?

I wonder if any of them have had sex yet. It's unimaginable.

If it moves into the other hand, Clark will have to learn culinary skills beyond just the grill.

Will I know when it's time?

King Cock

Austin doesn't know how Nick had obtained the key card to this first-floor room that's nowhere near Waukesha's AmericInn territory. He and Celery Sticks, whose name is Amber, are standing guard—or sitting guard, rather, their backs against opposite walls, their legs forming an M shape across the hallway.

"What do you think they're doing in there?" A stupid question, even as it's leaving his mouth.

"Probably nothing," Amber says. "Tina has a serious boyfriend back home. Plus, she's religious."

"Yeah, so is Nick."

Amber looks bored, and Austin knows he's letting an opportunity slip away. He hears giggling from around the corner and pulls his legs toward his chest. "Drawbridge," he smiles at Amber, who pulls her legs back too.

Two parents appear, Mr. and Mrs. Lodermeier, leaning on each other. But they stiffen and silence themselves as they see Austin and this girl they don't know. Grant's dad narrows his eyes at Austin, but it's more annoyance than suspicion.

They disappear around the next corner, whispering to themselves. Austin thinks about how Grant always puts his socks and T-shirt on before his boxers—and he makes a decision. He extends his legs again, squeezing Amber's Asics between his Shawn Kemps.

"So what position do you play?" she asks.

"Forward. Winger." Austin feels like he's chewing on a banana peel. "Right wing. What position do you play in volleyball?"

"Volleyball's not like that. We play every position."

A few seconds go by, and Austin doesn't know if they'd for sure transitioned into talking about sex. "What I really want to play is goalie."

"That's what you really want?" she bites her lip. "Isn't it fun scoring?"

The opening rhythm of "Enter Sandman" is the signal. Nick opens the door almost immediately. He's fully clothed and the room smells very dank.

"Hey Austin," his smile dopey.

"Amber!" Rice Cakes calls from the bed. Her eyes are red, but she doesn't look sad. Mary Hart is on TV.

Amber mouths something to Tina, then turns to Austin. "Maybe, the bathroom?"

Amber closes the door behind them.

Confused about logistics, Austin lifts her up and sits her on the sink. It isn't his first kiss, but it might as well be. Celery doesn't taste like pepper but it makes soups taste peppery. His brother had told him that you're supposed to kiss a girl for a while before you go for more. Just as he's wondering how long is long enough, Amber puts her hand up his shirt, her palm on his heart.

When he tilts his head for a new angle, one eye can see around her—to the mirror, to itself, to his hand disappearing into her dark hair.

Jay

Jay Gimberlin opens another Seagram's for his wife despite the swallow still in her current bottle. She takes it from him and goes through the act of twisting off the top without seeming to notice he'd beaten her to it.

"I'll ring their goddam bells."

"Just ignore them." Gone is his wife's charming bewilderment.

"I wonder which one's Fifteen's mom."

"Who can say?"

"The penalty should be castration. The ref should lead them to the penalty box, yank down their pants, and just get it over with. Look at them. Little volcanoes of testosterone. Little cavemen."

He takes the fraying coil of paper out of his pocket. It's memorized by now, forever, but he wants his eyes to verify its existence, the strangest indictment he'd ever received from a cookie:

YOU WERE BRAVER YESTERDAY

THAN YOU ARE TODAY.

Back at the restaurant he'd tried to let nothing show on his face, but still people needed to know.

Today's trials are tomorrow's victories, he'd improvised. His fake fortune, no doubt prophesying a Waukesha tourney win, received a rousing cheer.

"My testosterone levels are a little high tonight." He plays with the loose skin at her elbow. "I checked with the front desk, and there are vacancies. Just like Rice Lake—"

"What do they need a hotel for?" His wife is unfazed. "Most of them *drove their houses here.*"

"What I mean is that I'm feeling a little frisky."

"*White trash!*"

It's difficult to tell whether or not the Sun Prairie parents noticed, but they choose this moment to ring their cowbells. The fat woman who seems to be the focal point of his wife's ire leans her head back and screeches.

Gwen rummages in her purse and extracts her keychain. Its blaze-orange emergency whistle.

"Honey," Jay grabs her whole elbow.

But she turns to him, and he immediately wants her anger directed elsewhere.

"Our son could have been paralyzed. He could have *died*."

She stands and puts the whistle to her lips.

Sam

Sam's thoughts had just drifted into the first nonsensical terrain of the night—how an NHL stadium is never as big as when you step through the tunnel for the first time. It's the tunnel to sleep or maybe the same thing as sleep, until he's blared out of it by a Roenick blast—

No, a fire alarm.

He's fully clothed, socks too. All sweaty. He doesn't know this room. He senses a presence next to him and remembers everything except the fire alarm. The air's full of the smell of burning, but it's just their equipment. Jumping out of bed, he kicks the bars of a hockey mask on his way to the light switch.

Corey a circular mound beneath the covers—he'd have to be deaf to sleep through this noise. Sam yanks off the covers. Corey is curled into a fetal position, hugging his knees to his chest. After the Sun Prairie game, in an argument over whether or not Corey had any shampoo for Nick to borrow, Nick had told Corey not to cry. *Maybe when your mom gets out of jail, you'll have double the moms.*

AmericInn

In the parking lot, the hockey players and the volleyball players scout around for their respective teams. "It wasn't me," Nick tells his dad. "I know," his dad says, lighting a cigarette. Some of the boys—the rule followers, the fire drill all-stars—are wearing little more than they had on in the pool, and Bennet Roo is fashioning makeshift robes for his shivering son from an armful of towels. Mr. and Mrs. Hackbarth are having a discussion with their son away from the rest of the crowd.

Grant Lodermeier stands looking at the hotel with his parents.

Darren Lin stands looking at the hotel with his parents.

The Waunakee Lady Warriors cluster together with their coaches and chaperones.

The Sun Prairie parents have left their cowbells behind, are keeping what distance the parking lot permits from those Waukesha goons.

Austin finds his dad over by the other parents, but his mom isn't there. Had his dad even gone searching for him? He doesn't seem all that relieved. More like confused. Or, oh God . . . it's more like *disappointment*.

"Where's Mom?"

"Your mother pulled the fire alarm."

It just isn't possible. How could she have known?

"I'm sorry, Dad." It's never going to happen.

"She'll be okay." What if last time was the last time? "She was just looking for a bigger bell."

Wally Rufenacht stands looking at the hotel with his parents.

Patrick Dove stands looking at the hotel with his parents.

Corey Little stands looking at the hotel.

Confused seagulls circle the lot, and there's that ocean smell again, the hint of vast open space nearby. But it's been an icy winter, so maybe it's just the salt they use on highways.

Liam Ihrke sidles over to Corey and drapes his coat over his shoulders.

"Marco."

Corey sighs. "Polo."

Everyone's turned to the hotel as if hoping to warm themselves in the fire, but the only glow comes from each room's rectangle of electric light. The alarm sounds tinny and forlorn out here. And for a second it seems like the alarm and the approaching sirens are speaking the same language, are calling out to each other through the night.

Make/Shift

Deep breath. Find Marta in sea of mortarboards. Smile. Find speech team coach, Mr. Projasky, who insists on calling memory palace the method of loci. Watch your plosives. Four inches from microphone. Deep breath.

Tattered welcome mat, shedding like their tabby, Nanners, who kneads it daily as she lingers on the threshold of indoors, out. Printed in black across the mat, effaced by shoes and sunlight "Welcome: teachers, parents, administration, and Saint Xavier class of 2015!" Pause for applause, silly string. Pretend you can't hold back your smile.

Glass storm door. Entered house so seldom through front door you feel like a trespasser. Rural Wisconsin. Dad brags about not needing to lock the doors, is hoping, you suspect, for an excuse to shoot an intruder. Inside, an immediate mirror on the wall opposite, black backing a rash through silver. Immediately, you see "My name is Clara Gestberg, and I know some of you are very excited to hear me talk for the first time." Laughter, thank God. Crickets would have been a disaster. Nolan sitting front row since it's alphabetical, not GPA except for you and Chris, the salutatorian. Nolan laughing at the joke and you almost break deadpan it's such a gift.

Slink across grouted tiles to the kitchen where prayer cards of saints from funerals are magnetted to the fridge, the groans of which Marta imitates conversing with the submarine pings of the of the washer and dryer down the hall. Calm martyrs in mandorlas flashing lazy peace signs or pointing to their fiery, thorn-pierced hearts like What's going on inside my chest? *Pictures of Mom's friends' kids you've never met, barely room for the State Farm Insurance 2015 calendar. June is Arches National Park, Friday June 10th highlighted in orange.* "Classmates, the world would have us think that this is an important day." Another pause, this one to make everyone nervous.

Dad stationed on the couch with beer, channel-surfs past Parks and Rec *before locating a docudrama about Vince Lombardi.* "Uh-oh, I can see you all thinking: the gloomy girl's gonna get all April Ludgate on us." Kids laugh, parents are confused.

Framed picture of the outside of the house inside the house. Aerial view, the trees separating your house from your neighbors' are half the size they are now. Bulge of septic tank beneath the grass like a goiter, a bladder about to burst. Two fake deer attest to Dad's love of nature and killing it. Elbow of Rat Race Road veering off Propagation Way. "Hear me out for a second, and maybe I'll accidentally say something inspiring. Yes, the world would have us think that we're standing at a crossroads, that today—maybe as late as tomorrow or Monday—we will choose our careers, become adults, and start a family. Some of us are really jazzed about this idea. Some of us know what we want to do with our lives. Some of us are even trying to get a jumpstart on the family part." Thank God no one got pregnant this year, though the ripples of laughter are still a little nervous. Also because of the alphabetical seating, Jacquie can't sit next to Nolan. See her back with the Ys, her parachute gown powerless to bloat her curves. The popular girl who's always shuffling cards, doing card tricks and not caring that it's nerdy because she's popular. Shuffling boyfriends, too, once one goes missing.

Hallway, a gauntlet of pummeling memorials. Coat closet on the left you hid in after breaking the Palladian window with a baseball. Doorframe you tripped and hit your head on getting chased by your brother with Nerf gun. Twenty-four stitches. Bathroom on the right, site of nightly interrogations. Clay's room on the left, door closed like always. You linger on the threshold. Remember, don't go in Clay's room. "But some of us are less certain. Somewhere inside, we're all a little suspicious that we become suddenly different people once they hand us that diploma cover with no diploma in it." Hold up empty diploma cover. Swore you wouldn't, but find Mom and Dad in the crowd. Mom easy to locate, so tall it's like she's on a bleacher above everyone in her row. Dad's pride still tinged with anger that Mom made him wear his dress Carhartt.

Your room so close to your brother's you could hear him every night exploring himself. Open your door—Clara's door—and step unharmed into Clara's room, the room that's painted pink even when it's not. Tacked to your bulletin board, the acceptance letter from Wisconsin. "Maybe that's the problem. Maybe once I receive the actual piece of paper in two to three months—maybe then my new life will begin. But why does the world think we need all these arbitrary markers of new beginnings?"

Bedroom like the bedroom of an underfunded set designer who has never met a teenage girl but has had them described to him in some detail. Poster of a particularly bohemian Johnny Depp plunking keys on a run-down upright, Mom having objected to Johnny's cigarette but not Dad's cartons.

Imagine your brother sitting with Mom and Dad—no,

that's not where he'd be. He'd be . . . there, in that row of students whose last names all begin with G.

Draped over an open closet door, a scarf you got at a poetry reading when Dad shrugged okay to a night on the town with Marta. New Year's Eve last year. On your desk, a journal filled with your own attempts, fitful half starts and scratched-out epiphanies, palinodes for prior palinodes. Turn the page, read the only epiphany that might stick: "Graduation, birthdays, New Year's resolutions, the college orientation soon to be inflicted on us, every Friday afternoon or football Sunday or Monday morning for the rest of our lives . . . And pretty soon, a decade's gone by, and we're left wondering when on earth one of these supposed life-changing moments will actually change our lives."

Nolan sneaks a peek at his phone, and you're sure that whatever nonsense he's texting is purer poetry than this speech you spent weeks on. He'll strut up for his diploma cover, and every girl will wilt, except Jacquie who will simply remember what the bravest girls might dare to imagine.

Step into the garage. Mingled smell of oil and fertilizer and beer dregs. Solveig's room, Mom calls the garage. Fiskars everything hanging on the unfinished drywall panels like gravity's pulling from the side for once. Dad's entire lifelong supply of care drained by a pegboard on which each tool is outlined in black marker. One crime-scene 3/8" wrench, a permanent reminder of his boyish daughter's negligence. You keep telling yourself to buy a replacement. It would be so easy. Dad won't do it because the only thing better than a complete set is chewing his disappointment. You'll never buy a replacement because you only think of it when you're in the garage or your memory palace's garage. Because you think about your father as seldom as life will allow. Sports Illustrated *poster of Solveig at a vineyard, clutching grape bunches over her bare breasts. Transform your parents' Dodge Ram and Town & Country into giant smartphones, see if you can get Nolan to pay back a modicum of the world's attention.* "We tell ourselves: maybe if I buy the iPhone 25, or start doing yoga, or move across the country, or if I can just hold on till the next Batman reboot . . . But the excitement the world promises us—it's impossible to maintain. Crossroad after crossroad after crossroad, and we begin to suspect that we're being distracted from something, distracted from truly transforming ourselves into the type of people who consistently pursue what satisfies us in life."

Your history teacher in the front row with a stopwatch, ready to clear the gymnasium and fill it with foam if your speech goes one second over. Spot Nate and Dave and Jordan, rounding out your brother's infield, a camaraderie that even alphabetical seating is powerless to disrupt. Jordan, the only boy you've been with. Sleepover sneak-attack because it was time to find out. Down in Dad's man cave, you hoping the idea of a boy having sex with a girl was erotic enough to let you forget that you had to be the girl in the scenario.

Step back into the hallway. On Clay's closed door, a metal sign: "There will, of course, be big decisions and momentous days, both happy and sad. Many of us will have kids, will get really awesome jobs, will get married. And none of us can avoid our share of tragedy in this life." Uh-oh. The gymnasium tenses, as if reverting to its athletic use. A thousand people wondering if the valedictorian would mention her vanished twin brother. Had they taken bets beforehand? *On Clay's closed door, a metal sign:* DANGER—RAY'S

ROOM—DISASTER AREA. *On Clay's closed door, a metal sign with a typo you only dare correct mentally. Like on your birth certificate: "Clara" instead of "Clay"—and the "F" a failing grade. Put your hand on the doorknob. Draw your hand away. Ray's or Clay's, you promised not to enter this room ever again.* "But this whole crossroads thing is still very suspect. The crossroads are every day. Every day, we decide to what extent we're going to be the exact people we want to be, and to what extent we're willing to compromise."

Instead, head down into the finished basement. Man cave minus the man because usually Dad's too tired to walk downstairs. Beer mirrors and neon pub signs, a pool table that slopes slightly—Jordan's thrusting hips—to that far pocket, mute chorus of mounted heads.

Jacquie chewing gum you know is spearmint. Sometimes she wears a toothpaste stain guys joke about. You discovered why, observing her perform rites of marijuana exorcism in the bathroom before homeroom. Jacquie doesn't know that humans can brush their teeth with their mouths closed. Pick a card, any card, and you pull my heart out every time. Checks her phone, and you know it's Nolan texting her: whens this dike gonna stop talking.

Stationary stationary bike, stationary weight bench and dumbbells. Xs on the dartboard chalkboard proof Dad once played cricket with you back in 2009.

He's just texting about a party. Stop torturing yourself.

Lots of autographed green and gold. On the hulking, accusatory flat screen, naked dragon momma. "Some of those compromises eventually pay off. You take an unpaid internship that lands you a job you love. Now you have money for the essentials, food and shelter and HBO Go, so you can keep watching *Game of Thrones.*"

Unfinished section of basement directly below your bedroom with radon detector and sump pump that wakes you up most every night. Woman cave, unfinished. Mom quilting at her sewing machine, shelves of plastic bins of CHRISTMAS, STUFFED ANIMALS, RAY TROPHIES. *Above those joists, Ray's room. Clay's room.* DISASTER AREA. *Glowing.*

Many of these faces had been the tines of a vast rake untangling the scrubland and corduroy fields of eastern Wisconsin for weeks last September, searching for boy. Seeking what they hoped not to find. These faces had offered their meed of hope and determination to Ray's dad and tall mom and awkward sister and hot girlfriend. Faces trying to decide if this sudden vacancy in their lives was potential lost lamb or prodigal son.

"But, make no mistake, some of those compromises are venomous. Are fatal. Are life sentences."

Back upstairs to the dining room where Dad sat you down after finding you on your brother's bed in your brother's boxers and socks, handle of beloved mini toilet plunger, an ersatz boner for a makeshift boy. This was it, the moment you would tell him everything, the moment you would inform him that their quota of grief had not yet been met. But you let him talk, let him try to figure it out unaided. Your cheek numbing back to life, you understood that "some sort of incest thing" was Dad's preferred explanation—and that you were going to let the moment pass without correcting him. You just kept staring at the distressed wood sign Mom had hung on the wall above the sideboard, blessed *in loopy script.*

Can Jordan stop thinking for

one second I had kind of weird sex with this girl? It was so fast he might not be sure it even happened. Had your brother ever found out? Found out his first baseman had made it all the way to home plate with his twin sister? Since that night, remembering that night, you've imagined yourself Jordan, imagined yourself Nolan's hips, Ray's hips, imagined Jacquie yourself. After I saw you in half, wiggle your toes at the audience.

"The way I see it, a lot of these milestones are just millstones. They're for the world's benefit rather than our own. The world wants to categorize us, to make a labeled inventory of our passions and beliefs and personalities."

Memory palace hatched line was supposed to veer right, to where your parents sleep, to the conclusion of your speech suspended in the boredom of a bedroom. Blah blah hard work, blah blah never lose sight of where you came from, blah blah pun on the double meaning of "commence," and you can't remember what else. You're already in Ray's room—now Clay's room, now and forevermore. You're breaking the promise you made to your mother, your huge flightless bird of a mom, that day she came home already in tears: you wouldn't mess with his things, wouldn't set foot inside his room, wouldn't touch his doorknob or linger on the threshold. Any threshold. Ray's exit, when you first realized that you are Clay, not Clara—as if he'd died and part of his spirit leaped into you. A transmigration of desire, appetites. As if it wasn't the brother who'd gone missing.

"No matter how many unique people it produces, the world is convinced that if it just provides enough labels, it'll have something to call everyone."

Not his exit exactly, but his girlfriend's now uncertain status. For months having fooled yourself into thinking you were just jealous of Jacquie, her intimacy with this other half of you. But, transfixed by her grieving more than your own, you understood why you were thrilled and terrified that she and Ray might stay together, that you and she would one day become sisters.

"It's a lure, a promise that we'll make sense to ourselves if we agree to make sense to the world."

Understood why part of you hated Ray and needed him gone from this earth. Jacquie, let me comfort you. Jacquie, ventriloquize your half-views into my dumb mouth. If suicide, hated him worse, for throwing away exactly what you wanted. If suicide, terrified there could exist a pain worse than your own.

"The world is made very nervous by unclassifiable people . . ."

Marta, the only one who knows—about Jordan, about Clay—and knows that you've deviated from your planned speech. Her face an anxious gauge of the extent to which you're coming apart. In public.

Deep breath.
Reconsider.

The day isn't just yours, and a big spectacle would be less you than remaining Clara the rest of your life. After all, this is Wisconsin—the state, not the school. But fall semester will find you there, exploring the impossible kinship of Oshkosh and Madison, blueprinting a brand-new memory palace, all your own. "Today we've accepted a new category: high school graduate. Let's be clear, there are plenty of worse things to be called. But what does that label mean?" Marta relaxes. Marta, who thought you were confessing not just *to* her, but *about* her—because you should have been. You should love bestie Marta and not the hot girl. But you let the moment pass without correcting her.

Still in Ray's room. Clay's room. Clay's room and no one else's. You compromised, but you never exited this space. Crease in the palm of Ray's baseball glove he was always trying to pound flat. Smell of sweat and boy. Pictures of him and Jacquie at Six Flags, soaked from a water ride. One picture of him and you at a Packers game, and every time you saw it, you thought: a picture of me and my tomboy sister, Clara. "It used to mean that we were fit to be employed. But now it tells the world we're fit to earn further degrees that might one day lead to being employed."

There, Jill Endo, the last person to refer to you and your brother collectively as "the twins." Post-funeral, awkwardly. No *I* in twin, Ray used to joke when you had to share food or toys or attention. When by necessity desire was split in twain. "If the last four years have been worthwhile, it's not because of a line on your résumé or a piece of paper. Rather, we should ask ourselves, how have our teachers and friends helped us better understand the world and our place in it?"

Until the day you tried on his baseball caps to see if you had the same sized head. Holding back your hank of hair and trying to convince yourself in his closet mirror that you were identical twins after all. One hundred percent. Strutting like Nolan down the hall. Trying to come up with an explanation Mom and Dad would buy, why you'd cut off all your hair and stopped wearing makeup. Marta. Who doesn't realize that a friend can be too supportive. That empathy can verge into something covetous, something somehow more insidious than bigotry. "Have we started to see this complicated world as it is rather than how

it's been presented to us? To understand which aspects of ourselves need drastic maintenance versus those that only need to
be maintained?"

Reconsider. Compromised, but you can still sneak
it in there, speak that word in this air. Make a whole auditorium
bristle, cough in the quarry dust. You see the route before you.
*The next day: Would I fit into his jeans, his shirts, his shoes? His bed?
Began to imagine yourself Ray, then Nolan. Then yourself. Clay.* "Or,
harder still, how to cope with those aspects of ourselves that need
to change but simply won't . . . or that we maybe shouldn't want to
change, but do. But can't." *Spent longer and longer every day fitting
in. At first reading Ovid Book IX on his bed, pausing every two pages
to call yourself Clay, glancing at the pictures of your girlfriend Jacquie.
Running your fingers over the words that were written for you alone to
find two thousand years later,* "Why do I cite such things? Where am
I veering now?"

History teacher malevolently holds up a sign that
reads 1 MIN in red.

*Looking forward to the football game that night
when you and Jacquie would curl up together in a fleece blanket and
drink hot chocolate, and nobody would think that it's strange because
that's what boys and girls are supposed to do.* "In Mr. Projasky's
class, you might remember he was very adamant that we learn
to distrust the either/or argumentative fallacy. It's a famous
method by which the failure to acknowledge the complexity of
an issue is depicted as virtuous. It's a way to remove the middle ground, the gray area, the potential for compromise: you're
either with us or you're against us. We're good at spotting the
schemes of T-shirts and TV commercials, but then we let the

world convince us to either/or our very souls." Has anyone ever filibustered a commencement speech?

Eventually resigning, reviving Ray's laptop and reading significance into the search history he'd failed to clear.

Compromised, but you can still say it. Who knows to which classmates—maybe even parents and teachers—the word will ring like a bell? Saint X, you may open your eyes. Then they'll know. "To ask the night sky only Yes and No questions. To render our poetry in binary. Spiritual or atheist, red or blue, straight or queer, high school graduate or going nowhere, *nature or nurture; mother or mothered; father, enforcer; some girl, girlfriend; confidante, collector; valediction, malediction; household, threshold; disaster, area; brother or lover or self—*

Nepenthe

It wasn't that Jake smelled different to each person. Rather, there were simply no known odors convincingly similar to the boy's, leaving each person who came into contact with Jake Longaway to grasp for some familiarity that never approached reality. I brainstormed on legal pads and designed elaborate spreadsheets to try and unravel each nuance. Eventually I landed on this: to me he smelled like the air rushing through the slivered windows of my high school carpool's Pontiac on a brisk autumn morning.

But then, in the grocery store checkout or the mall food court, there he was—or there he'd recently been. Either way, the *actual smell* laughed at the comparative destitution of my attempts to pin it down.

I conducted a series of impromptu interviews with my fellow locals, asking for their impressions. Some were uncomfortable discussing the matter, and several had the nerve to claim that they did not know the boy, or, worse, that they had not noticed anything unique about his odor. A few of these naysayers even treated me like I was some kind of creep for asking the question, but they were few in number compared to those who knew exactly what I was talking about and were immediately able to produce answers like "the red, orange, and purple Skittles mixed together," and "hot apple cider at a football game," or "the hologram sticker inside a pack of baseball cards." Although these descriptions at first seemed unrelated, I did notice that they all tended to invoke childhood, nostalgia. For example, I see in my notes that Dawn

Van Persie likened Jake's smell to "a tent you've left too long in its bag and are now sleeping in . . . except pleasant." When I asked her when was the last time she'd been camping, she replied, "Oh, not for thirty years."

The Longaways moved to our town during a particularly cool August that gave way to a balmy September. They chose a house in the foothills outside of town, a house that had been on the market for half a decade due to its bordering a cattle ranch.

In every other regard, Jake was aggressively plain. His hair was dishwater brown, ditto his eyes. Freckles lightly peppered his face. He was of average height for an eleven-year-old, average weight, average intelligence.

We were never sure what exactly Mr. and Mrs. Longaway did for a living. Something with computers, they claimed, though we suspected they were independently wealthy. Dealing with their son's condition was probably a full-time job in itself.

This whole ordeal might have been averted if they had been stricter. Many parents, seeing the effect of their son on the general public, might have locked him in the turret, so to speak, or at least homeschooled him. But Naomi and Edgar Longaway wanted Jake to grow up normal, and they had a sense of rightness with the world that was all the more infuriating in that they had given birth to proof of the contrary. It's true that they attempted to suppress his smell. They bathed him in every cologne and odor neutralizer they could find. They draped him in heavy wool. They even tried tomato sauce.

They were not without rules regarding how their son handled his uniqueness. They made it clear to Jake's teachers that he was not to sniff himself in public, and they asked to be notified if he was caught enjoying his fame a little too much. For it was not a self-deception on our town's part that we noticed Jake had developed a proud strut, as if his odor was a plumage he was wont to unfurl. They could not entirely police these tendencies, of course; when they entered his bedroom to wake him up in the morning, they inevitably found him fully under the covers, curled into fetal position, like he was trying to hoard all of his smell for himself.

They did not allow Jake to participate in sports. We knew nothing of his life before arriving in our town, but a rumor began to circulate of a soccer game in which the other boys gave up chasing the ball around the field and started chasing Jake. A new variation on the popular sport—soon the referees, flaggers, and parents joined in. It was not hard to imagine. Whether or not the gossip held a shred of truth, Jake did not go out for the soccer team that fall. A doctor's note released him from the hell of junior high gym class, the unstated reason being that any exertion on the part of Jake intensified the scent.

On Valentine's Day at Jake's school, he, like everyone, brought in a decorated shoebox with a slot cut in the lid. Unlike the other boys, his box was so full by the end of the giving session that the lid would no longer stay in place without hands holding it down. Sweet-smelling cards had been popular the previous year, and local stores had stocked up on them only to find that nobody wanted them this time around. Most of the girls and some of the boys insisted on making their own cards that year, laboring for hours in hopes to come across as attentive but not needy, mature but not unspontaneous.

This incident was only one in a series of indications that our town was attempting to purge itself of all odors aside from that of Jake Longaway. The perfumer we brought in later confirmed a baffling consumer trend that had been noticed as far away as New York City. It was not unusual, he said, for sales of perfume and cologne to rise and fall based on the popularity of whatever celebrities attached their names to the labels. But for an entire town to suddenly stop buying these products entirely . . . Air fresheners, potpourri, and scented toiletries grew stale on the shelves of grocery stores. The gardening culture of our town—which had several times been featured in regional publications—cut back on flowering plants in favor of tall grasses, ivies, and succulents. We didn't want to be distracted from the memory of our last good whiff. Other smells were embarrassed when they came within close proximity to Jake. Their artificiality and other shortcomings betrayed their gaudiness in his presence. If you couldn't smell Jake, it was better to smell nothing.

Animals were unaffected by Jake's smell. Cats were particularly disinterested. Though the odor from the Longaways' house mitigated the smell of the ranch next door, the cows themselves acted neither grateful nor perturbed. Jake did not attract bees or repel mosquitoes.

Jake's first year here was a good one for all of us. The ghost town of our river district bustled with hat-tipping and flag-waving. Previously floundering students started outshining their reputations. Businesses boomed—except the perfume counter at Begley's, of course. Our high school, which seldom amounted to much athletically, had a stellar year, with boys taking first in wrestling at states, and the girls track team breaking several records. Jake did not have his own float at the Fourth of July parade—but he should have.

After about a year, though, there was a subtle regression. A hazy disquiet nagged the collective mind, and I think it was this: our town's relationship with Jake was not going to change. Sure it would be interesting to watch him grow up, to try and detect subtle changes in his scent. But what if he matured into a dull, unimaginative young man? Or what if his scent was so tied to youth that it vanished during adolescence? The worst scenario of all, however, went unarticulated in the minds of most: that he would grow into a perfection that matched his odor, that his odor might even mature exquisitely like an aged bourbon—and that he would then leave us. If we could convince him to attend our modest community college, that still would only delay his inevitable departure by one or two years. We knew our town could not contain him. Still one further level of the unfathomable: another city would experience his smell, would proudly claim it their native resource, as had some other forsaken wasteland a mere year ago.

Then, thank God, a scapegoat presented itself. Clancy Grannis was a seventy-one-year-old retired electrician who had been living in our town all his life. He'd married his high school sweetheart and raised three sons, all of whom had excelled in school and who now raised families of their own in other cities. Clancy played golf three days a week and low-stakes poker on Saturdays. He had quit smoking years ago but still enjoyed bottomless-pizza-and-beer night at the VFW. On the morning of the impropriety, he was volunteering as a crossing guard near the elementary school. "Just to make sure I get out of bed," he winkingly told people.

A crowd of students was crossing with Jake, so there was no lack of witnesses. When asked at the trial to describe Mr. Grannis's demeanor, Jemina Bowles said, "He looked like he needed to go to the bathroom." His stop sign trembling, his eyes darting over the group of children, he spotted Jake. As I wrote earlier, the boy was more than accustomed to his local celebrity, but he told the jury that this attention seemed different: "A dog right before it growls." Jake quickened his pace. The children heard a clatter as the stop sign fell to the asphalt. Mr. Grannis caught up to Jake, carried him to Jo Horkin's front lawn, held him down, and pulled off the boy's shoes. Jake barely had time to scream before Mr. Grannis had pocketed his socks and hurried off.

The climate toward Clancy Grannis on the first day of the trial was chilly. A crowd gathered outside the courthouse—an old structure that dominates our quaint town square—and yelled insults as the police escorted Mr. Grannis from the awaiting squad car. Someone threw what turned out to be a handful of clothespins.

Jake was not present that day in court, but he was brought in on day two to describe the strange attack. The mob was placated by the smell that continued to blossom outside after Jake was led through the front door of the courthouse. The jury smiled distantly, Judge Hoogenraad rested his gavel, and Mr. Grannis struggled to the point of tears not to relapse there in front of everyone. The prosecuting attorney, Felicity Sujek, immediately sensed her error—but didn't seem too upset with herself. The effect was obvious—having the smell there in front of us, cooped up by the old building's terrible ventilation, made us all very understanding. How could we condemn Mr. Grannis when all of us were fighting against the same urge? Derrick Rajala called himself as a spontaneous witness in Mr. Grannis's defense, admitting that, as Jake's barber, he saved every towel he used to line the boy's collar.

Jake's family exited so that a sober ruling could be arrived at:

Mr. Grannis would quit his volunteer position as a crossing guard and never come within smelling distance of Jake—we joked about a "restraining odor"—and the trial quickly turned into more of a town hall meeting dedicated to confronting the issue. The idea we came up with was that, if an artful enough fabrication could be concocted, the city could administer the unction as a harmless enough substitute for those who, like Mr. Grannis, required one.

One voice of dissent quieted everyone's self-congratulations. The man who stood up was Frank Okurowski, our local black sheep. The older among us had watched him fail to grow out of a mischievousness that had, in earlier years, been charming because of his youth. Alcohol led to drugs, and he lost the job his late father had secured for him in construction when the police raided his ramshackle house on a tip that he was cooking. In and out of prison, he could be found most days, bottle-in-bag, at the bus stop near the Books 'n' More. What seemed to be the most benign of Frank Okurowski's addictions, nasal spray, had completely destroyed his sense of smell.

He'd tried to make himself presentable that day. Come to think of it, none of us had seen him at his usual outpost for at least a month. Maybe he was getting help. No amount of soap and water could remove the lines that hard living had carved on his face, but his hair was clean and newly clipped. He wore a turtleneck and gray slacks with black dress shoes. Murmurs coursed through the courthouse—but not too loud. We would hear what Frank had to say.

"People might be tempted not to listen to me because I've made so many mistakes in my life." His words were memorized. "But for just a minute, look at it a different way: I'm an expert mistake maker. A virtuoso. Maybe I'm the most qualified person here to diagnose this fiasco we're all taking part in."

Some people were already done listening, and began to make this known.

"And I'm not alone." Five individuals flanking Frank Okurowski stood in solidarity. There was Dr. Yonkus, an anesthesiologist, Rabbi Rosenbaum, Father George, Dawson Ammer, a local playwright and renowned debauchee, and Lizzy Sykes, Jake's math teacher. We found out later that a seventh was supposed to stand—Claudia Milner, a marriage counselor—but that Jake's proximity had overwhelmed her resolve.

"Sympathetic I most certainly am," Okurowski continued, then pointed at Mr. Grannis, "but this man attacked a boy. He has committed a crime."

"Another area of expertise?" Felicity Sujek jabbed. Some laughter, some applause.

"Absolutely," Okurowski nodded. "And as an addict, I know that the only way to gain control of yourself is to remove the temptation."

The room was sickly silent at the idea's implications. "And how do you suggest we . . . remove this temptation?" Judge Hoogenraad asked the obvious question.

Dawson Ammer answered: "By asking the Longaways to leave our town permanently."

Our town government approved the proposal to bring in an adroit perfumer from New York City. A prim, fashionable, humorless man, he supervised the unloading of his U-Haul at the Gaslamp Inn, including a giant chest and a moon-shaped white desk with four tiered shelves. A perfumer's organ, we soon found out the desk was called. The chest yielded nearly a hundred corked vials on each of which was written, in a spidery hand, the captured scent.

Mr. Castel—that was the perfumer's name—requested to see Jake privately in his chambers, but of course Mrs. Longaway would not allow this, and so Mr. Castel permitted her to accompany Jake under the condition that she thoroughly bathe beforehand without soap or shampoo, and that she wear clothes that likewise had been cleaned without detergents. Mrs. Longaway assured him that she was not currently menstruating. She also agreed to leave several articles of Jake's clothing in his keeping.

Then, three months of silence. Mr. Castel had his meals delivered to him in his room, and his only other contact with the outside world were couriered packages to or from New York. A cartoon in our local paper showed Mr. Castel in strung-out, romantic isolation, focused intensely on his scale and set of weights. The caption read "Maybe a pinch of salt." Finally the *Gazette* released, in a front-page story, the news that Mr. Castel had successfully reproduced Jake's odor, and would uncork his masterpiece at a gala event to be held in the town square the following week. Everyone was invited. Two days later, though, the *Gazette*'s printed cancellation of the gala dampened the excitement and preparations that had been building since the announcement. Though the story claimed that Mr. Castel had been forced to return to New York due to a nervous breakdown—which might well have been true—we knew that the real reason for the cancellation was that Mr. Castel had tried out the scent on a test group of locals and had met with downright hostility. We knew this because I knew this—I was in the test group.

The smell was ninety-nine percent the same as Jake's—but instead of that one percent becoming lost in the cologne's over-whelming success, it seemed to mutiny against the smell, becoming more and more accentuated, until that one percent was all you could smell. That one percent was my high school carpool having bought some cheap cigarillos instead of his characteristic cloves. I asked the others in the test group what that one percent smelled like, and here's what we agreed on: phoniness, disrespect, vulgarity, a pinch of salt.

Everyone in town did eventually get to sample Mr. Castel's creation. A bigwig in the New York perfume business purchased the recipe at an exorbitant price and marketed it under the name Nepenthe. A teenage pop star attached his name to the label. Everyone's initial reaction was outrage that our Jake had been commodified, that our town's proud secret had been suddenly disseminated worldwide. But we laughed off our outrage when we discovered that the fragrance was an impostor, that our secret was safe. Some speculated, however, that the whole test group and the release of Nepenthe was a complicated ruse. Mr. Castel's senses were too attuned, his perfumer's organ too formidable, to have failed at his task. They hypothesized that the real Nepenthe was a secret being kept by the government for the purpose of subduing large groups of agitators, or possibly that the bigwig was selling it at an extreme price to only the millionaires who could afford the real thing.

Jake's family moved out of our town under the cover of a cool autumn night—for of course that is how this story was always going to end. The next morning, I leaned out my bedroom window to clip the out-of-control ivy that risked twining its destructive way into the window's mechanisms (it grew at an amazing pace overnight, latching onto my newly painted trim with alien tendrils), and I was struck by an absence. Like everyone in our town, what I noticed was a lack of noticing. People poured into the streets, morning cup of hot lemon water in hand, to discuss why we all felt that this day was going to be different than the ones that came before it. Many of us skipped work.

News came down to us of the for-sale sign in front of the Longaways' house. We were all plunged into a mutual agony that we all knew had to remain private. We had lost Jake Longaway because we had not been able to control ourselves. A bidding war ensued, and by noon the house had sold for three times its value to the richest man in town, Avery Capaldi. By two o'clock, a security force was in place guarding the property. By the end of the week, a chain-link fence crowned with concertina wire had been thrown up around the house. By November, an inflatable dome. Avery had been a very social man, and could be found most nights at O'Fallon's, but from that day forward he secluded himself in the Longaway house, and all claims to having seen him around town came across as desperate and hazy.

Jake's scent was not the only absence that vexed our senses. With him gone, we all realized how bland we had allowed our town to become. It was completely scoured of smells, of personality, of flavor. Some panicked, thinking that we had all lost our powers of olfaction. A suggestion from one of Jake's classmates sent many of us to the nearest gas station, where we slopped the rainbow liquid onto the pavement and breathed deeply of an odor both brand-new and distantly familiar. We uncovered other smells as well: at the neglected arboretum's Compass Rose, at a bakery that had managed to stay open on Main Street, in the cluttered drawers where we tossed the detritus of school supplies. I raked my front yard and burned the leaves.

People dealt with the pain of Jake's departure in their own ways. A week after the Longaways' flight, our town experienced its first suicide in over fifteen years when the six-foot-four center on the high school basketball team, Ben Zale, hanged himself. As he did not leave a suicide note, we couldn't prove that his death had anything to do with Jake, and we were left to attribute it to the teenage angst felt most acutely by those who have the least claim to it.

Some pursued more constructive answers. What started out as clandestine self-help groups quickly mobilized into quasi religions. The Beholden believed that Jake would one day return to the town and reward them for their faith. They held daily meditation sessions. They continued to purge their life of, not just odors, but of tastes, textures, and music. They sabotaged our paper mill. They looted any stores that sold Nepenthe and even attacked residents who cloaked themselves in what they called "The False Idol." A splinter sect of the Beholden, the Beckoned, believed they needed to "go out into the world" to search for Jake Longaway. They had Mr. Castel working for them from New York City, feeding them the numbers on fragrance sales worldwide. Any time a precipitous plummet occurred, the Beckoned would hurry to the destination. "But most of all," one of the Beckoned told me, hoping to convince me that their faith was grounded in more than just consumer trends, "we follow our noses. The nose knows." That was their mantra. Others, energized by an evangelized Frank Okurowski, used the continued failure of the Beckoned to argue that the Longaways had not been flesh-and-blood humans at all, that they existed in the realm of the supernatural. A final group— much more shadowy and nebulous—had only one goal: to locate the real Nepenthe fragrance withheld from us by Mr. Castel.

Most of us, however, retreated silently into our daily routines, buoyed by the new wealth of local odors we began to rediscover.

But sometimes when the wind kicks up—or when it dies down completely—we swear we catch a whiff of Jake Longaway, possibly borne off a tree he climbed with friends, or a glove he left beneath a park bench. Or maybe Nepenthe has begun to fool our forgetful noses. Either way, we breathe deeply and remember. And momentarily we forgive ourselves—for everything.

Let's get to work

Then they died, and it turned out the afterlife was just like the duringlife. The poor were still poor, the cripples were still crippled, the whites were white, the perverts were perverted. And graduates of the University of Phoenix still had the skills necessary to succeed in today's competitive marketplace. Most of them realized they were dead, but nobody could say if they were in heaven or hell and which religion's version. By which I mean, let me be clear:

everyone knew, but no one could say.

Because I Can

With the rise of the sun the place is abuzz, preparing for today's version of going forth and returning. You do the daily dance, stuff yourself with enough energy to power your body until its next hiatus, groom yourself and your family, communicate your hopes for the hours ahead. The daily dance, you swing your body into the driver's seat, the seatbelt seeming to buckle itself, the garage door to open of its own volition, the vehicle to sink down the driveway and shift directions without any conscious movement on your part. You fly off, to Whole Foods, eager to feel good about where you shop. After making all the familiar turns, however, you find yourself in an unfamiliar part of town, no closer to your favorite grocery store. Compelled to walk into a random office building, you find that the door is locked, your coworkers gone. It's neither the weekend nor a holiday, but several other businesses that share the office building with the company you may or may not work for are likewise closed. You begin to wonder if some calamity has been visited upon the outside world, bringing a halt to the workday, and you reach for your phone to ask the hive mind what's up only to find that your pocket instead contains three poker chips and one of those despised devices that lights up and vibrates when your table is finally ready. You suck down the rest of your Diet

Coke—because you can—and walk back out to your car, tonguing the syrupy residue that has collected in the space between your teeth and lips. Not sure of where you are, you plug the nearest Outback Steakhouse into your GPS and follow the calm voice, certain that all desired answers await you at the red pushpin. Destination is half a mile ahead on the right, *the voice tells you, but now you are out in the hinterlands, driving on a rutted maintenance road that grants access to the vanishing point of humming power lines. You are very hungry, night is falling, and you can't remember how many children you have.*

Arrive at destination. *Ahead of you on the right is the corner of a room and a pile of bodies. You know they knocked against shuttered glass until their last reserves of power were drained and they fell to the empty shelves, certain that here's where home should have been.*

The best part of waking up
is Folgers in your cup

Blinding white sixty watts, it squints like the first lungfish flopped from the ocean, inanimate objects consciously hostile: sensible wardrobe hides in closet wilderness, mattress inches forward every night, deranged alarm clock flies off again, inexplicably. The best part: doing so alone. It checks the mirror to make sure it's still young. Sometimes it can't tell dreamed from did. It can't recall a single plot point of the last episode it watched last night before surrendering. On its coffee table, the evidence of battle. It knows the worst part of waking up is waking up. It has been told, "Whatever ritual keeps you sane." But bacon on the stove, Folgers in its cup, hangover pending, its social in a network, it begins to understand—begins to understand—it begins

The Buffalo Zoo. An elephant kneels toward the snow, straightens back up, kneels and straightens over and over. The boy is delighted by the dance—its father, a doctor, less so: "That's dangerous boredom. You see it in humans too."

Muscle Memory

"You type fast."

Barbara looks up from the desk computer where she'd been typing a student's travel plans into the dorm's running log.

"Maybe you should be a typist or something."

"Morgan, I don't think there are many available positions for typists, seeing as this isn't the 1950s."

"But you can't be a hall counselor your whole life."

"I've only been a counselor for—" Barbara pretends to consult a mental calendar. "Three months."

"But what about next year? What's your plan?"

Morgan's advice is hardly given in the spirit of helpfulness. She's currently upset with Barbara because she'd kicked her and three friends out of the piano practice rooms at the customary lockup time of 10:30.

Now it's past eleven, and Barbara announces to the lobby that it's time for everyone to head to their rooms.

Morgan doesn't budge from her stool. Students can sometimes stay up later if they're talking to a hall counselor, and Barbara decides that—although she aches to be done with students for the day—this is alas one of those times. Maintaining order in the residence halls without becoming a villain often means easing off of one rule while sticking to another. She'd already strong-armed Morgan and friends out of the practice rooms, so Morgan can stay out here the whole night for all

Barbara cares. Getting sent to her room in annoyance would be a victory for Morgan anyway.

"I mean, you don't want to get stuck at this job again next year," Morgan harps on the topic, "living with a bunch of teenage girls. It's not normal."

"I don't see myself doing this job forever, but until I figure out exactly what I want to do—"

"Aren't you a little old for that?" the eighteen-year-old asks the twenty-six-year-old.

Barbara decides against changing the subject, instead hazarding the heartfelt: "Morgan, some people spend high school and college deciding what they want to do with their lives, but some of us aren't so lucky. We spend college, maybe grad school, maybe the next decade figuring out what we *don't* want to do with our lives."

Morgan gives Barbara's speech zero seconds to sink in. "I've known since I was seven years old and my parents took me to Ravinia. I'm going to Curtis and I'm going to be a concert pianist."

Yeah right, Curtis. "I don't mean to sound condescending, but I probably would have said something similar at your age."

Morgan scoffs at the condescension regardless. "So you had your chance, you didn't do it, and now you have to make a new plan. What do you want to be?"

"Counseling your counselor, huh?"

"You're not *that* type of counselor." A wrist motion flings away the silly idea. "You're more like a summer camp counselor who had nowhere to go in the fall."

Barbara repeats to herself a mantra that Blake Sikorski, a fellow counselor and a bit of a guru, had coined: *If you find yourself in an argument with a student, you've lost.*

"What you're saying could be construed as not very kind."

This is quickly turning into one of the "five really difficult conversations" her boss Janelle had warned them about during orientation week.

Barbara stands. "I need to go do a hallway check. Want to come with me?"

For the first time tonight, Morgan is caught off guard. "Um . . . no. I should be getting to bed. The concerto competition is soon, and I have to play the Grieg for studio tomorrow."

As the hallway door closes behind Barbara, she gasps like she'd been locked in a trunk underwater. She sinks down against one of the cinderblock walls and pulls at her hair. She's losing control of her hall. It isn't just Morgan either. Even though Barbara treats students decently and has committed no major blunders so far, she imagines that everyone is beginning to see through the "illusion of authority" Janelle had also spoken of, seen through it to a directionless twenty-six-year-old girl puddled on the floor of a dormitory. These kids are so stupid sometimes that she forgets they're some of the smartest kids in the country.

By the time she finishes roaming the wings and returns to the desk, her fellow Tuesday night closing shift deskmate, Jan, has returned from wherever she'd been since sending the students to their rooms.

"How's your night been?" Jan asks.

"Great."

The word slipped out, automatic—but it felt true. As Jan plays a game on the desk computer, Barbara sorts through the conversation with Morgan and the impasse of her third decade on earth in an attempt to diagnose the unwarranted confidence she feels rising within her, the night's hidden momentousness. And once they've closed up the desk and she's retreated to the foxhole that is her bedroom, she's figured it out. A way to wrest back control of her hallway.

Instead of changing into her pajamas and passing out with a horror novel, Barbara goes to the bookcase on the wall above her bed and pulls down a stack of sheet music. She's looking for a thin, cyan-colored book, the cover of which had unstapled itself under the strain of so many frantic page turns.

Gargoyles—Op. 29—for Piano—Lowell Liebermann

She opens the book, and a shiver warns her to close it back again. The shiver isn't only her physiological reaction to seeing this particular arrangement of musical notes on staves. She feels a numbness needling her hands, gauzy gloves being pulled off by the fingertips. Her stomach hits a sour chord, holds it.

And it doesn't leave when she closes the book, doesn't disperse when she lies in bed. It keeps her awake for an hour or more, trying to name the daunting bigness that has returned this night to stalk her.

She tries to tell herself that there's nothing she can do about it until the morning. She herself had locked the practice rooms for the night.

The good pianos, the mostly in-tune Steinway grands, are located in the new Argerich Building, but those rooms are hard to come by. Plus, she's loath to deny one of the nice rooms to a student who might need it.

More importantly, her task requires secrecy.

With a backpack full of books, Barbara descends to the

basement of Graham Hall. Two international students are studying at a table in the common area. Melodies and chords from various instruments squawk down two hallways.

The students turn back to their studying. Barbara would
rather no one have seen her at all, but these two aren't much of
a threat. She hurries past the doors of a horn studio and a harp
studio, hoping that their occupants won't have the chance to scru-
tinize the passing figure.

Some shy student had taped staff paper over the window on
the Everett practice room's door, a self-conscious measure that
does not bode well for aspiring musicians—but one that suits
Barbara's present purposes. In its prime, the Everett piano had
been at best serviceable, but now it sounds like a honky-tonk house
piano. Sitting down on the too-high bench, she removes all the
books from her backpack. She should start with an easier piece,
maybe the Mozart sonata she'd played sophomore year, or some
Hanon exercises. After all, she hadn't played in a while. Since grad-
uating, she would have an occasional bout of renewed interest in
the piano that would last maybe two months—one thing she had
never done, however, was return to *Gargoyles*.

The page is bloody: the mechanical precision of the printed
music versus frantic penciled notes. The numbers one through
five attempt to negotiate tricky runs and awkward chords. Pedal
indications, practice suggestions, bookmarks she can return to in
case of disaster, a diagram that shows exactly how five notes in the
right hand line up with three in the left. Vagaries: *Memory, Cohesive
line, Ghost Notes, Don't speed up—Now you're too slow, Don't shorten*,
and the unmincing *GET IT RIGHT*.

The gargoyle of the first movement is a furious imp, winged.
It stamps out maddening three-versus-five polyrhythms and jams

seven notes, ten notes, into a meter designed for six. When it rains, this gargoyle directs its runoff at children and the elderly. In the final three measures, it flits away, pride wounded. In the end, a trifling bully.

The gargoyle of the second movement is hulking, dull, and slow-witted, but beautiful in its melancholy. There is something wrong with this gargoyle. The others mock it, call it sight-readable, flaunt their virtuosity. This gargoyle can't tell the difference between C major and C minor, so it plods between the chords while the upper register tries to find the right thing to say.

Perched on a church, the third-movement gargoyle catches glimpses of the painted cherubs inside and, at night when everybody's asleep, strikes their poses. It too has wings, but no feathers—sometimes it fashions a halo from a wire hanger and pretends it rules the light instead of the dark.

The third movement snags Barbara. Don't *think* about the fourth gargoyle yet, even though it's number four that packs the fireworks that will drop Morgan Unwin's jaw. The wannabe angel has called to her, and she begins dusting off its *moto perpetuo* sixteenth notes, tossing them from left hand to right and back. The right-hand pinkie speaks the melody. The first thing angels always tell people: don't be afraid. Like Barbara's mind the last twelve hours, it's prowling epiphany.

Since page one of a piece is usually what you learn first, it stays with you the longest, and Barbara's idle years drop away as she runs it with no big blunders. On the second page she begins to slow down, begins to need to look more and more at fingering that makes less and less sense. Halfway through the second page, the gargoyle scrambles to the spire of the cathedral in a series of recklessly leaping arpeggios, and Barbara's musical connection

with five years ago vanishes. The gargoyle shatters on the flag-
stones of the plaza.

It's then that she remembers: she had stolen *Gargoyles* from
Max Malvern.

Of course she hadn't forgotten Max.

She looked back on her four-year obsession with her classmate
as a dark, dangerous, shameful detour in her life. It had embit-
tered her toward her time at the University of Montana, toward the
college experience in general. Nor had she actually forgotten her
theft of Max's repertoire. But she'd forgotten the disaster's daggers,
its stamina—the sleep deprivation, the constant anxiety over his
whereabouts (his *whoabouts*), the drone buzzing in her stomach.

Max was one of those people so lost in himself that he could
be looking at you, talking to you, without ever actually thinking
about you. Like a cat that knows its name but would rather clean
itself. It was to a dog, though, that one of Barbara's sympathetic
but baffled friends had compared Max: a stray mutt with a dustpan
for a face. "He even has a dog's name." Probably the dustpan was
Max's freckles, a facial feature Barbara had never considered her
type. Nor his black hair, usually long and inclined toward greasy,
parted like a jagged scar above his left eye. His face was all cheek-
bones and lips, distracting you initially from his dark, dark eyes.

Barbara first met Max in the place that would become, for the
next four years, their unavoidable common ground and the stage
for Barbara's fits and soliloquies and night vigils—the piano practice rooms in the music building. She doesn't remember the why
or what of the conversation, probably just names and repertoire
and gripes about the school's pianos. But what she does remember
is the feeling of no-real-reason giddiness that lingered long after

she tried and failed to turn back to her music. No, it had a reason. Here she was just a month into college in this sublime place, and already circumstances had brought her into early friendship with the only person she would ever need.

She had dated in high school, had had crushes, had thought that these feelings were what everyone was referring to when they used the word love. And maybe they were. But this miracle seemed completely private and original. It was in watching him eat. It was the rare occasions he got a haircut. The way he fell right for stupid gags in TV commercials, laughing himself to tears at things that weren't very funny. His jumpiness—he was once memorably startled by a broken string during the *Mephisto Waltz*. He yanked his hands off the keys like he'd been electrocuted and looked up at Barbara and burst into laughter.

Other humans go their whole lives without experiencing this, Barbara was sure. Otherwise, love would be more famous than it already is. Tell me, have *both* people ever felt this way? No, that would be a force too powerful. Divorce would not exist. Feminism would be unnecessary, misogyny far less rampant.

In the end, the both-people problem was the problem. Barbara's happiness lasted most of freshman year, marked by days of confusion over why she and Max weren't together, over why the one planet necessary for an ultrarare alignment seemed to prefer spinning in isolation on the other side of the solar system. She flirted; he didn't notice. It seemed logical that she would have eventually worked up the courage, but she wasn't simply some girl with a crush. She was one of Max's few close friends, his best friend. With their history together, a date could not be casually suggested. That possibility had disappeared long ago. Only a complete confession would do.

By sophomore or certainly junior year, the joy had burnt itself out. It was now the happiness that was intermittent, hectic ecstasies of misinterpreted smiles, conversations that could almost fool you into believing they were as good as what they weren't. That was when the nerves and the jealousy moved in. Not jealousy of a rival; in Max's four years at Montana, he did not date and did not have any intimate contact with another person. Barbara was quite sure of it. Such an encounter could have persuaded Barbara to do something ancient. No, she was jealous of anything Max gave his attention to, whether it be his roommates, those television commercials, or his instrument.

Often it was just the two of them lighting lonely windows on the second floor of the music building. The two nicest pianos were in neighboring rooms, and the wall dividing them was not completely soundproof. She knew Max's repertoire, where in each piece he struggled. When frustrated, Max would hammer a few bars of Khachaturian's Toccata before resuming his work. The drop-in was the highlight of Barbara's night, though often she wouldn't be able to wait for him to initiate it. Then some nights she would suddenly notice a silence, her stomach would play that dissonant drone, and she would realize that Max had left the music building without saying hello or goodbye. She envisioned him tiptoeing past her door so he could escape without having to talk to her. Then her gut would tell her a scarier story: he'd simply forgotten. Cue the darkest piece in her current repertoire.

Barbara had originally wanted to minor in music at Montana, but she soon found herself practicing five hours every night, planning her junior recital, learning the Rach 2. And it wasn't for her career's sake. Nor her love of music. Music, in fact, had become an ambivalent substitute for the tangible. Often Barbara despised it. Music allowed her a sham access even as it barred her full entry.

She'd chosen Missoula primarily for its location. She'd been an avid hiker, canoer, and rock climber, and a certain movie starring a certain blond-haired actor with no freckles had long romanticized the state in her mind. But she soon found that the sky in Big Sky Country is smaller for the bigness of the land. The surrounding mountains began to make her feel like she was gaping up from the bottom of something. She stopped exploring Rattlesnake, stopped planning weekend trips. Instead of an exciting, wild frontier, Montana became a desolate tract of earth wandered by dazed exiles. Missoula's isolation, its always eventual winter, fortified the jagged walls and sharpened her inescapable proximity to Max. Nature had become furniture. Most absurd of all, the giant *M* on treeless Mount Sentinel loomed as a reminder of the life that throbbed somewhere below its switchbacking tourists.

Other people, in that they weren't Max, became trifling and clownish to Barbara—and she let them know it. Not through outright meanness, but rather by imitating Max's supreme self-absorption. She started pretending that she didn't hear people when they said her name. She forgot birthdays. She failed to RSVP, failed to show up. She stopped noticing when guys flirted with her. She would volunteer to sober cab and then get drunk on purpose.

Every night when she lay in bed, her fantasy scripted a new reason why Max had been unresponsive to her wiles—and why he could remain so no longer. But she could only come up with three real possibilities. One was that he didn't love her, but she generally thought of it thus: men do not love. Sitcoms and the weddings she'd attended supported this hypothesis. But the piano music she wrestled with every night was a stronger counterargument, the male of the species's capacity for depth.

Two, of course, was that Max was gay. Barbara had once schemed a pizza and movie night to which she'd invited both Max and a very charming gay confidante. Tyler confessed that his gaydar had registered not a single blip.

Hypotheses one and two were terrible but bearable. Three was that Max had once felt for another person what Barbara felt for him, that his self-absorption was not self-absorption at all, but rather a constant meditation on this figure from the past. Next to such a pyre, Barbara knew that she would come across as just some girl. To Max she would be no different than the dozen or so guys over four years who had attempted to thaw her out. As she heard his Schubert through the practice room wall, her greatest thrill was hoping that he had her in mind as he played. But what if . . .

Barbara feared Max's indifference more than anything else, so there was a dismal pleasure in making him feel anything—including confusion, disappointment, and anger. At a school as small and noncompetitive as Montana, it's bad form to learn a piece of music in the same year as one of your peers once he or she has already laid claim to it. Maybe nobody wants to know for sure who is the better pianist. Because of the pride at stake in exhuming a unique composition, this etiquette is intensified if the piece is obscure or contemporary. Liebermann's *Gargoyles* is both.

Barbara discovered Max's discovery one day when she snuck a peek at what he'd been playing on Spotify. Barbara went online and overnighted the sheet music. Showing up to the music building earlier than usual the next day, she'd already begun taming the third gargoyle by the time Max arrived.

He opened the door of her practice room without knocking. He looked more like the gargoyle of the second movement, the plodding, speechless one.

For a moment Barbara wanted to continue being a good devotee—if not to confess everything, then to at least assure him she had no intention of playing it for her senior recital. But she'd tried for three years to be a good devotee, and the frustration Max was trying not to show was the closest thing to love she'd so far moved in him, the smallest dose of a turmoil akin to her own.

She'd practiced her response over and over in the small mirror on the wall of the practice room. You're playing these? "Yeah, I've always wanted to."

M is for mine.

"I've always wanted to," she says now in the practice room at Andermatt Arts Academy as she starts back at the beginning of the third gargoyle. Don't forget. Ever again.

She'd forgotten the night she lay shaking on the floor of the women's bathroom in the music building, filing her nails on the filthy grout. She'd forgotten the pep talk she gave herself in the mirror most nights. *Survive. The only goal of senior year is survival. You can botch your recital, fail all your classes, and it won't matter as long as you keep breathing. Because, in a few months, you'll escape.*

And she had escaped. Once she graduated and left Montana, she slowly began reintroducing herself to herself. Herself before Max, herself after Max, herself as though Max had never existed.

The next morning, Barbara skips breakfast again and heads down to the Everett room. She'd practiced for six hours yesterday, and now most of the third movement is back under her fingers. It's strange how muscle memory works. Barbara looks at a string of notes, the fingering, and everything seems unwieldy and foreign. Then, moments later, she forgets to think about it, and her hands just go there. There's something grotesque in the hands' independent knowledge, a dormant virus. It's like the atavistic alarm at seeing a snake or spider, except it isn't inborn. It's the creating of new instincts. If ever she had children, would a ghost of the knowledge be passed on?

She'd controlled herself admirably yesterday, sticking to just the third movement. But today, after an hour of continuing to chip away at number three, her hands flip to the fourth movement and launch into a few sloppy measures of hand-wrenching triplets. *Presto feroce.* Number four is an army of gargoyles—two armies, rather—marching, fighting, dancing. They're engaged in a reverse tug-of-war atop an island butte. One gargoyle army surges forward and forces their foes to the edge. Impossibly the foes rally, go on the offensive, pushing their stunned enemies to the opposite edge. Each time, a few gargoyles tumble off the cliff, some of them forgetting they have wings. The weather itself loses its patience with the squabbling horde, sends down lightning bolts that split the ground asunder. Both armies are flung laughing into the ocean below.

Here Barbara is greeted with one of Rene Ghirardi's mementos of frustration. At the most difficult moment in the piece, where ascending octaves in the bass land on four monster chords, her irascible teacher had written *TENTH!* This in reference to the right-hand interval Barbara often had trouble locating. Rene's handwriting impaired by his fury, it reads more like *TEETH!*—and this word used to blare in her mind every time she approached this hazardous section. These teeth had bitten her badly at her senior recital.

She turns back to the third movement.

She should have known something was wrong just by the "Taste of _____" food served every Thursday for lunch, the whole table of fellow counselors she finds sitting together.

There's an open seat by Ezra, who for some reason is dressed business casual. They'd been flirting with flirting as of late, Ezra and Barbara, spurred on largely by inaccurate student gossip. Barbara likes Ezra, likes him enough to say yes were he to ask her to dinner in town. However, now that she'd recalled Max, any feelings for Ezra are laughable by comparison. Even as she sits down next to him and offers a smile, she internally flaunts and wallows in her lack of real affection for this young man.

Ezra doesn't return the smile. Had she broadcast her mean thoughts to him telepathically?

"Where were you today?"

"Huh?"

"Today's Thursday."

Oops.

"We figured you weren't feeling well," says Jan. "In fact, you're not looking so hot."

"But still able to put away a hefty helping of pot stickers," Ezra razzes.

This comment would have bothered Barbara had she not just mentally trumpeted her indifference for Ezra. This is how students must feel when dragged into a disciplinary meeting; the faces are attentive and concerned.

"I'm fine," she says more curtly than she should have. She

turns to Sofia Messer, the residence life manager of Graham Hall. "I'm really sorry, Sofe. I just completely forgot until right now. I haven't been sleeping well lately."

"You are in soooo much trouble." Her boss feigns graveness, shaking her head.

Once the intrigue over the absent counselor has died down, Barbara turns again to Ezra, taking the daintiest bite possible of her General Tso. "Ezra, I was thinking we should put on a counselor recital. You used to play the clarinet, right?"

"I like to think I still do," he replies, chewing. "You know, because I still can."

"Dani, you play guitar, right?"

"Yeah?" Dani burns with the shame of talent. "But it's not very impressive unless I'm singing. And then still not very impressive."

"Shut up," Blake tells her. Then, to the table, "She's awesome and she'll do it."

Dani sighs. "There goes any respect I might have been cultivating."

"Anyone else?"

"I can burp the ABCs," Blake grins. "In German."

"We'll save that for the encore."

"I play the harp," offers a quiet counselor named Molly Novotny.

"What is this, *Quartet for the End of Time*?" Barbara says, and only Ezra laughs. "I'll talk to Other Barbara and see if we can reserve a space."

"I didn't know you play music."

"Yes," Barbara replies, "I play music."

* * *

It's sixty-three paces from the Everett practice room to the east stairwell. Barbara lugs open the heavy fire door and ascends to the first-floor hallway. Only the most unbalanced young women on campus can call themselves members of Jan's hall, a.k.a. "the Ward." Barbara takes sixty-three steps down the grimy industrial carpet, and of course it's Sissy Scioro's room. Barbara has been secretly resurrecting *Gargoyles* beneath the dorm room of the biggest gossip and best pianist at Andermatt.

Barbara had first become suspicious earlier that morning when she observed not Sissy but one of her stooges, the once-sweet Emma Simmons, lurking around the Everett room. Barbara passed Emma with a nod, pretending she was on routine recon. She decided to delay her practice session by an hour, but when she went down again after breakfast, a second stooge, Nicole Hisong, had come to relieve Emma.

Sissy is staking the place out.

Not that Barbara has much to be embarrassed about at this point. Gargoyles one through three are fully rehabilitated, and number four is on its way. But the counselor recital is only two weeks off, and Barbara doesn't want to be discovered until then. After that she can practice wherever the fuck she wants. Her work on *Gargoyles* had slowed down somewhat since she'd agreed to play the first movement of Brahms's E-flat clarinet sonata with Ezra and Messiaen's two-piano *Amen des étoiles* with Frank from IT. The fourth movement is beginning to show its belly, but it still nips her once in a while with those *TEETH!*

For now, to avoid Sissy's lackeys, Barbara moves to a piano in the basement of Gatsby House. She's not as worried about the boys spying on her.

* * *

"Whoever it was didn't show up today."

"I thought you said she was like clockwork."

"She was. Every day, same time."

Sissy and Morgan are speaking in conspiratorial tones as they sign in at the desk for the night. Morgan is a girl struggling with her weight and her plainness, but Sissy is the opposite. Or, rather, she's having the opposite struggle. Too pretty, too thin, her hair dyed blonde and bobbed hatchet-sharp at her jaw. Done signing in, they step aside.

"Have you figured out what piece it is yet?"

"No. None of us know it. Turns out Shazam doesn't work too well through asbestos. Maybe Rzewski."

Not Rzewski. Good guess, though.

"Could it be a nonmajor?"

Sissy shakes her head. "No way. It's too good for a nonmajor. It's one of us. Some weasel that wants to surprise us at the competition."

Barbara can see her own reflection in the computer monitor, and her smile is fiendish. She focuses her hearing through the lobby's loudness.

"*It's a concerto?*"

"Sounds big enough," Sissy replies.

"Who're you sending tomorrow?"

"Same girls. I told them I'd tell everyone it was them who narked on Tracy."

The girls pass back by the desk on their way to the Ward, and Morgan makes eye contact with Barbara, smiles. Hard to believe just a few weeks ago she'd been afraid of this girl.

Then again: Had Barbara been made to hear this conversation on purpose?

* * *

A knock on the door, and she immediately mutes the Bruins game. But she knows it's too late; the volume had been up too high. Since it's Barbara's day off, she's fully within her rights not to answer the knock. As the laminated sign on the door clearly advises, *Students needing assistance should speak with another member of Residence Life.* But the student knows that she's in her room, that the room's sudden, aggressive silence is bullshit.

Telling herself that maybe this knock heralds a question that can be answered with a simple yes or no, Barbara relents and stands and opens the door.

Morgan. This would not be a yes or no.

Morgan bites her lip. "Hey Barbara, I know it's your day off, and I'm really sorry to bother you, but the concerto competition is tomorrow, and I absolutely *have* to run the Grieg one more time, and I was wondering if you could accompany me."

Worse than Barbara had worried. The counselor recital is next week, the gargoyles all bottled up and antsy and ready to be sprung upon a delighted audience. Slopping her way through an orchestral reduction in front of the student she most hopes to surprise is a less grandiose coming out than she'd hoped for.

But the climate between Morgan and Barbara has been changing the last few weeks, with Morgan swallowing her acerbic cattiness and at times acting downright chummy. And Barbara senses now in Morgan's demeanor a clumsy attempt at genuineness, or at least a deft fabrication.

"Maybe." Barbara hesitates. "The building's full of pianists. Can't you cajole one of them—"

"All the ones good enough to sight-read are practicing their own concertos."

Barbara counts to three. "I can try. Hopefully my stumbling through it won't make things worse for you."

There aren't any practice rooms with two pianos in the Graham basement, but a few of the studio instructors have given students permission this week to access their offices. The studio of Dr. Landeta, a horn teacher, has a lot more personality than normal practice rooms: a paper-strewn desk, dusty rugs, and more horn-related comics taped to the wall than Barbara would've guessed existed. Morgan sits at the grand piano and Barbara at a Boston upright. Barbara opens the second piano score and channels what little arrogance she possesses. "Whenever you're ready," she says, not a glance at the music. Morgan looks taken aback, but she closes her eyes, draws a few deep breaths, and nods.

"What did you think?" Morgan asks after the final mighty chords. She's trying to bite her lip as before, but a grin is peaking through. She knows the answer to her question.

"I think you might win," is the required answer. The necessary follow-up, "And if you don't win you'll still be proud because your interpretation is spot-on." And "I loved how delicately you resolved the cadenza," an appropriate detail.

The grin unbites Morgan's lip. The bite quickly recovers. "Do you have any suggestions?"

If Morgan had asked this question two weeks ago, Barbara could have provided her with several. But not the night before the competition. "Musically, no. But, for the nerves, I used to recite a few lines from *Hamlet* right before I walked on stage: 'If it be now, 'tis not to come; if it be not to come, it will be now; if it be not now, yet it will come—the readiness is all.'"

For once, Morgan seems to take the time to process the words said to her. "I'm not totally sure what that means."

Barbara laughs and Morgan laughs. A release. The nerves are still there but they recoil from the laughter.

"We'll abridge it to 'Readiness is everything.' And you just showed me that you're ready."

There are tears in Morgan's eyes, and Barbara now understands that they're not from laughing so hard. There's a box of tissues on the piano (probably for just such performance hysterics), and Morgan wipes her eyes.

"I want to win," she starts slowly, "but not for the usual reasons. I want to impress somebody. A particular somebody."

Barbara thinks about telling Morgan that she herself had dropped her physics major and shunned all fun in college just in order to impress one person with her piano chops. But it isn't her time to chime in just yet. Plus, Morgan doesn't want anyone to be able to relate to this dilemma. She wants it to be personal and unique.

"Do you know what a gay boyfriend is?" Morgan squints and cloaks the question in doubt—as if it were riddled with inscrutable jargon.

"I've heard of this phenomenon."

"Well . . ."

Justin Kirkland. A motion picture arts major.

"And we're best friends, and we tell each other everything. Every time he sneaks into Brandon or some guy's room he tells me all about it. And I have to help him through all the drama. And all I want to do is . . . is to *be* his drama." Morgan pauses, frustrated that she can't articulate the mess without sounding like the teenage girl that she is. "What a lame, stupid thing to say."

"Love is never stupid." A lie.

"You kid yourself into thinking that, if you're just . . . *around* the person enough, then that would be sufficient. But very soon it's not enough. Not nearly. And it's made everything worse."

Barbara pretends to start to speak, to stop herself, to start again. "I know right now it seems that there never has been and never will be anyone other than this guy. But the good news is that, despite the bad press, there are some pretty good heterosexuals out there."

"Out there." Morgan groans. "Maybe. Exactly. High school is supposed to be the best time of your life, but there's twice as many girls as guys at Andermatt, and half the guys are gay. I'm losing years of life here."

Try only having ten to choose from, Barbara considers her male coworkers. "Even if you don't find a guy at Andermatt, you're building up experiences that are valuable in a different way. And college is only half a year off." Barbara—who'd gone those four years without being touched.

Embarrassment curls a tight smile on Morgan's face. "I didn't really need to run the Grieg again. I guess I just needed an excuse to talk."

Barbara thinks that this just might be one of those "five life-changing conversations" that Janelle had predicted during orientation week.

"Any time." She returns Morgan's smile. "Just try not to think about him when you're playing. Nothing makes a performance sound less passionate than passion."

Taking the stairs two at a time, Barbara figures she can still catch the third period of the—

Uh-oh: Morgan had just informed a figure of authority that

another student has been breaking a pretty significant rule. Is there any way that Morgan loves Justin enough to hate him enough to get him in some serious trouble? Does Barbara now have to talk to Justin's counselor?

Can't you have one wonderful conversation with a heartbroken student without immediately scouting for ulterior motives?

No. Never again.

Although Fintan Turek ended up winning the concerto competition with the help of J. N. Hummel and a bassoon, Morgan still looks happy afterward. She'd played really well, Justin had been there to see and hear it, and at least her best friend Sissy hadn't won.

Barbara hadn't taken her own advice.

It's the night before the counselor recital, and a grievous misstep has destroyed her focus. She's been staring at the piano keys for several minutes, and the precise sequence of countless tiny movements it takes to successfully produce notated music seems a laughable impossibility.

Nothing had provoked the phone call. She'd just been up in her room watching TV when—

No, it was a television commercial. A Geico commercial with woodchucks. So stupid, but those woodchucks would have set Max laughing harder than any joke Barbara could have labored over.

It was muscle memory, hands knowing what to do without consulting the brain. The phone was ringing, and already it thrilled her that maybe this ring had caused a reaction on the other end of the line. Maybe Max had to stand up to get his phone. Maybe it buzzed on his thigh. Maybe he smiled when he saw her name on the screen.

"You have reached the Sprint PCS voice mailbox of . . . *Mmmmmax* . . . To leave a voice message, press one or just wait for the tone. To send a numeric page, press two now." The most despised of pauses. "At the tone, record your voice message. When you are finished recording, you may hang up or press one for more options."

"Hi Max, this is Barbara . . . Halvorson. I was just calling to say hey and see what's up. I'm playing *Gargoyles* in a recital tomorrow, and it made me think—"

Someone answered the phone, and Barbara realized her facial expression was like she'd been talking to Max in person.

"Hello?"

A woman's voice. Not a girl's voice—the one Barbara had slipped into botching the voicemail. A woman's voice. Just one word, a customary greeting, but still it had some distinctive quality. Boredom? No, boredom is too close to arrogance. That voice: excellence.

Barbara's thumb found the red circle, and her stomach immediately remembered it hadn't hit that sour chord lately. Like Justin Kirkland to Morgan, Max's indifference was only tolerable if Barbara could convince herself that Max had dismissed the whole gender—or species. He was supposed to have suspended himself in a vacuum until the time they would meet again. Barbara had. It didn't really matter that the excellent female could have been any number of nonromantic figures in Max's life. In twenty seconds, Barbara had ceded her tormentor a significant foothold, and that tormentor would brush away five years of hale apartness and recovery. It would whisper in her ear that Max had finally found the forbearing infatuate who had rendered Barbara just-some-girl during all of college.

Their daily life together is opera. They have no friends, because friends are a distraction. They try not to leave the house.

Tonight's entertainment will be Barbara's abortive voicemail, played and replayed. They will snatch the phone from each other, laugh as Max tries to recall the repressed girl he'd watched movies with back in undergrad.

Now, back down in the Everett practice room, Barbara presses the sustain pedal, tensing the space with the metallic non-sound of the strings' readiness. No walking to another building tonight. Since the recital is tomorrow, she doesn't really care if her secret is out. In order to attract the desired crowd (in particular, the snotty Graham Hall musicians), she'd had to do some promoting. So everyone by now knows that she's playing *something*. The Liebermann, the Brahms, and the Messiaen are all in top-notch shape, but she's still having problems with the very end of the fourth gargoyle, those teeth disguised as tenths. She hears a gargoyle version of Rene Ghirardi screeching *TEETH!* every time.

She begins with a practice technique that involves starting at the measure before the trouble chords but only pantomiming the leap without pressing the keys. Each time her fingers tap the keys, she says "TEETH!" out loud. She plays it over and over, a looped track.

"TEETH!"

"TEETH!"

And it doesn't matter how often she reminds herself: nothing makes a performance sound less passionate than passion.

"TEETH!"

The need to remind *is* the passion.

"TEETH!"

"TEETH!"

Her fingers landing true each time.

"TEETH!"

This time she'll play the chords. And as the sixteenth notes race toward the two-handed monster, she knows she now owns it forever . . .

"TEE—!"

She yanks her hands off the keys and turns them palms up. She stifles a scream. Two fingers on each hand have struck blood. The blood does not look so out of place on the white piano keys. A red carnation pinned to a lapel. One key has failed to fully pop back up, caught on the safety razor inserted between it and its neighbor.

Barbara's heart throbs in her fingertips, and for a moment she does nothing to staunch the bleeding. She stares at words written years ago, *Ghost notes*—when a key is pressed, but not forcefully enough to make a noise—and she allows her vision to go out of focus.

It gets in your hands; it gets in your guts. And it never leaves.

Enough Sealant to Pool
the Concavity

March 12th

Most evenings I go for a short walk around the neighborhood, my route always the same. I take a right on 1st, another right on S Street, uphill three blocks to where it Ts with 4th, east two blocks on 4th along the Calvary Cemetery, then back to 1st via U Street. Last night was my first walk since Bri's death, and I wondered: Why such a cemetery-centric route? My circuit could just as easily staircase south toward Reservoir Park, where students from the U play Frisbee and parents admire their kids from playground benches.

Here's how Wikipedia describes the grid I call home: "First surveyed in the 1850s, the Avenues became Salt Lake City's first neighborhood. Today, the Avenues is generally considered younger, more progressive, and somewhat 'artsy' when compared to other neighborhoods. Many young professionals choose to live there due to the culture and easy commute to downtown."

I used to think about death constantly—that was during my religious teens . . . I was going to insert a verse from the Bible here, something along the lines of "Always keep in mind your last days, and you will never sin," but those memories are so distant and the internet is so crowded with sin and warnings about sin that Google's divine algorithm is powerless to help me locate the quote. I saw my classmates doing what teenagers do and—how could they just ignore the punishment in store? Even if they didn't believe, wouldn't they at least be wise enough to acknowledge *the chance* that the fire was real and gamble on the side of avoiding it? As those fears gradually then suddenly receded, as I realized that disbelief could be active rather than passive, I experienced an unexpected side effect: my new certainty that everything would go black when I died alleviated my fear of death rather than intensifying it. There was nothing I could do about its inevitability, so it wasn't worth thinking about. I could be decent just for the sake of being decent.

These brief recollections risk flashbacks I'd rather avoid—I admit I wouldn't be recording them if not for my employer-prescribed grief therapist's insistence. If not for my fear that neglecting to do so would suggest that I've inadequately grieved my daughter's death. I keep myself very busy, and I'm not sure that time off work is really going to be beneficial. I haven't had time just to sit and think in years—and that has suited me fine.

During my walk yesterday evening, I noticed for the first time the abundance of crack sealant on 4th. The other roads in the Aves are not so heavily sealed (I had to check), making me wonder if 4th is more heavily or less heavily trafficked, better kept up or worse. I got a few strange looks for photographing the asphalt, particularly because I have a dumbphone and my only means of taking stills is a video camera.

I found myself groping for a metaphor, the sealant as a labyrinth, as intestines awaiting divination, but it escaped me until I passed by T Street and saw painted on the asphalt what I momentarily mistook for graffiti. Since I couldn't read it, I found myself tilting my head, then walking around the graffiti so that it would be north of me, thus, said my logic, legible. Strange logic since the Aves reads bottom to top, 1st being the southernmost street, a grid radiating outward from Temple Square.

What appeared to be ornate black writing highlighted in white turned out simply to be the coincidental crossing of street sealant with the strip of white paint alerting drivers where to stop at the intersection.

Writing, it occurred to me. The street sealant is just like writing.

I mean, the white line is no doubt a type of communication. Although I'd never given any conscious thought to the semiotics of road surface markings, it says "stop here" just the same as the white letters on the red octagon. I inspected the sealant lines more closely. The beginning was a mess, a snarl of capital *R*s and *A*s and *Y*s. Then a sort of *W* or *M*, a cursive *R* and the number one. A zero with a slash through it (Greek phi or theta), a *T*, an *A*, a *P*. Trailing off into maybe a *Z* at the end.

I think my anxiety over starting this journal, of writing something for the first time since a college creative writing class, something that doesn't have to do with projecting city water supply, must be causing me to see writing everywhere. The power lines themselves sag and crackle with communication that only my dimness keeps me from deciphering.

March 13th

Last night, my route was disrupted by the appearance of a stranger headed north on U Street. My feet just started following him, along the eastern edge of the cemetery. I tried to stay far enough back that I wouldn't arouse suspicion, but close enough that I might get a good look when he passed under the streetlights. I wanted a face to paste onto my absurd fantasy. There was no reason for my heart to be pounding so hard, for me to feel the thrill of the hunt. He entered a house and was greeted, I saw through the window, by a kitchen full of twentysomethings holding cans of beer. Hanging back, I wondered what the reaction would be if I knocked on the door, asked if it was an open party. I had never visited this section of the Aves on foot.

March 14th

I set out again last night searching the dark streets for Bri's lover. It's crude to think this way—my daughter's death as a liaison—but my mind ignores all pleas for decency.

I know that my chances of encountering Bri's lover are slim, but it wouldn't be the most remarkable coincidence this winter. I brought along my camera, not sure if it would work in the dark or what I'd do if it did, and devolved into a species of creature more dependent on its ears than its eyes, filtering the night's hush for a sound that's familiar even though I can't remember ever having heard it other than in movies. Suctionless unstoppering. Metal that's heavy.

As I walked by the cemetery on 4th, I noticed a little neon

light that someone had used to decorate a loved one's headstone. It was a meager flare in the night: red to purple to blue to green to yellow to red to purple to blue to green to yellow to red to purple to . . . A dismal vigil, and I found myself thinking: if I'm to be remembered thus, I'd rather be forgotten. Regarding my cremated remains, my instructions will be *Dump wherever*. I've always liked Zion National Park and could see my ashes borne from the peak of Angel's Landing. But it's such a popular destination that there'd be people all around who'd get bummed out. Also—the thought was there before its stupidity could dawn on me—I'm afraid of heights.

Above the cemetery, the letter *U* luminescent on a hillside, blinking: red red red red red red red . . . It could stand for Utah, Utes, or University, but my mind transformed it into the pronoun. Zoom out a miniscule distance (proportional to the cosmos)—the grave's little light and the bombastic *U* would be equally invisible.

March 15th

I told Rich in our session today that inactivity is not helping with the grieving process, and he suggested that I take up a hobby or two. We decided on Nintendo and piano, both of which have been sitting inactive in the house since Bri's death. I used to play piano, but I never really got into video games. Also, whereas the musical instrument is unchanged since the last time I'd played it (and for two centuries or so before that), the new Wii U system Bri'd brought into the house had evolved into a radically different beast than the gray console on which I'd last chased a one-up mushroom down a bottomless pit, much to my friends' delight. The hulking controller alone threatened to overwhelm me. It had its own screen, and everywhere a finger might rest there was another button or joystick. The first game I fired up was called *ZombiU*, not the diversion Rich had been imagining, I'd imagine. It took me an hour to get past the game's intro, a weaponless character fleeing zombies through a subway to get to the safehouse, following the instructions of voice that identified itself as Prepper.

The safehouse contains: 1) a metal locker where you can stow weapons and ammo and health packs that you pick up on your missions across embattled London, 2) a work table where you can add modifications to your weapons, 3) a computer system that provides you with surveillance of the game's various districts, 4) a generator you have to refill with fuel every so often, 5) a bed where you regenerate as a new character when you die—I find it's best not to get too attached to any single character, and 6) a manhole cover you lift off to reveal the entrance to the sewers. *ZombiU* inverts the sewer system into a place of speed and safety, allowing you to warp at loading-speed between the safehouse, Buckingham Palace, Brick Lane Market, etc. The surface overrun with verminous versions of *Homo sapiens*, the previously proximal space between civilization and its subconscious has become a haven for what traces of humanity remain.

March 16th

The presence on Bri's desk of this vintage toy:

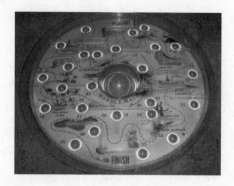

The goal is to negotiate a ball bearing from the START alcove around a maze of plastic partitions without allowing the ball bearing to fall through holes in the surface that represent a variety of hazards: Haunted Mountains, Black Mountains, Blood Lake, Man Eating Plants, Poison Desert, Tiger Valley, Sargasso Sea, etc. I spent twenty-three minutes playing it before finally reaching the FINISH, a cramped and boring haven.

March 17th

Today Rich asked how my grief documentation is going, and I told him that I have nothing to write about.

He told me there's always nothing to write about. I'm not sure how clever he was intending to be.

I'm auguring snarls of tar sealant, I told him. I'm stringing Bri's status updates on telephone lines. I'm reading everything I can find (without moving from my chair) about the Well of Souls.

Not a natural cave per se, but a chamber beneath the Foundation Stone, where Abraham purportedly attempted to sacrifice Isaac and/or Ishmael. But cave-like—but *inside*—a chamber further interiorized by the Dome of the Rock. Pierced Stone. Wikipedia: "Jewish tradition views it as the spiritual junction of heaven and earth." I tried curling into a ball in the deepest corner of my unfinished basement, but it wasn't the same.

March 18th

In an effort to learn how to better use the controller's touchpad to navigate postapocalyptic London, I stumbled across a *ZombiU* promo video online that demonstrates its various functions. The hands holding the controller get increasingly twitchy as the three-and-a-half-minute video progresses. The viewer is not sure why. At the video's conclusion, the arms' veins and arteries blacken, its flesh molders, and—if that isn't enough—an off-camera screech testifies to the game's infectious capacities. It's a clever marketing scheme, and accurate in different ways than I think its creators foresaw.

March 19th

Bri's birthday. I don't drink very much except tonight. Made the mistake of going on her Facebook page and scrolling through the birthday wishes and her final posts. In my current disbelief system, the continued persistence of her Facebook and Twitter and Instagram and Pinterest pages are the best approximations of a soul and the afterlife that we can attest to. The first step in the science fiction scenario of being able to upload our conscious-nesses and live forever.

I unfriended the friends who wished Bri a happy birthday without knowing that she'd plummeted to a lonely death. Now only twenty-one people like her "suicide" post, down from the initial forty-two. Police and logic eventually ruled that her death was not suicide. It was an unlucky night, and sometimes you just happen to vaguebook right before you die of what passes in the forensic community as natural causes: *Wikipedia is heaven when you don't want to remember no more.*

Lo, Google informs me I've been quoting Bri quoting Nick Cave. Sweep me away for an hour or five, Wikipedia, you means of discovery and forgetting to which I return again and again. Give me discography, give me *Murder Ballads*, by God give me personal life.

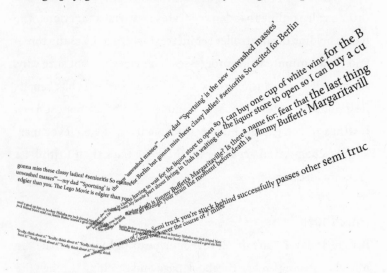

March 21st

One infuriating aspect of *ZombiU* is that, when your character dies and you regenerate as another character with another name and former occupation at the safehouse, you lose all of the resources that were in possession of the character who died. That zombified character's location is marked with a skull on the map, and if you want your weapons and ammo and health packs back, you have to go to that location—now armed only with a cricket paddle, a handgun with six rounds, and whatever you were wise enough to stow in the safehouse's locker—and fully kill the character you'd been trying so hard to keep alive. If you die again before doing so, all those supplies are gone.

Discomforting, what comforts us.

Not only does my bedtime get pushed back further and further each night by my urge to meet *just one more* of the game's objectives, but the game's content, graphics, and geography are corrupting my daily perception. I begin grafting the face of Arthur, my daughter's lover, onto the zombies I clobber or shoot or incinerate. I bring a crowbar on my patrol one night. I imagine access to a sonar map of the Avenues in which I am the locus of radiating pings and my daughter's boyfriend is an elusive red dot. Manholes, too, are marked.

I begin expecting the infected to pop out at me, and I scout for escape routes. I see a section of the fence around the cemetery that has been displaced, and I gauge whether or not it's enough space for my character to fit through.

I love how the post topples in segments, in super slow motion. The way wrought iron gives way to chain-link. The mysterious symbol on the third block from the bottom—in *ZombiU*, I would scan this symbol with my gamepad and it would provide me with a clue to a clue to a clue that would lead me to Arthur, my daughter's lover.

March 22nd

We are infected. Twenty years ago I taught my hands a Chopin mazurka, and these past two weeks my hands have taught it back to me. It's so strange how much knowledge lives on in us unacknowledged, atavistic/instinctual or just part of our daily ballet. I reached a level in *ZombiU* called Ron Freedman's Flat, which includes a room where you have to pick off zombies that have been lulled by the nepenthe of throbbing bass and black lights. Even though they're not technically alive anymore, their bodies remember actions they performed during life and respond automatically to stimuli.

Trying to memorize the Chopin, my brain will alert me to a difficult series of upcoming measures. I'll be fine now, fine now, but I'll feel the approach of chord or ornamental figure that I know will trip me up. And it will trip me up, and I will go back to one of my bookmarked measures and start again. But that chord or figuration is not content to simply remain resistant and rotten; it will spread its clumsy amnesia backward to meet my oncoming fingers. I will greet the dementia a measure earlier than before, rewind again, get tripped up two measures before the first time. More and more of the piece will fall into darkness until I end up admitting forfeit and bringing the sheet music back out so the whole mazurka isn't engulfed.

I worry that all memory works this way. For example, I'm confident in my general memory of our "therapeutic" family trip to Zion the year before the divorce, or Bri's reluctance to move back in with me when she didn't get accepted anywhere but the U. But then I try to recall details from those scenes—the words of a conversation, what we ate for dinner—and my inability to do so taints the whole year of life with such unreliability that I'm left wondering if it ever really happened.

March 23rd

This morning I awoke to find the city workers applying sealant to the section of 1st right in front of my house. Behind their truck they pulled a giant orange tank streaked with tar and dirt, and I wondered about the similarity in temperature and consistency of this sealant compared with the tar used in the defense of castles in the Middle Ages. Google: tar or pitch, along with stones, hot sand, molten lead, and boiling water were dropped on enemy soldiers from "murder holes," holes in castle ceilings, barbicans, or passageways. Google: tar is more or less fluid, depending upon its origin and the temperature to which it is exposed. Pitch tends to be more solid.

My mind moved to treasure seekers combing the beach sand with metal detectors as I observed the workers tracing their wands over the asphalt in cryptic glyphs. Wikipedia: "The simplest form of a metal detector consists of an oscillator producing an alternating current that passes through a coil producing an alternating magnetic field. If a piece of electrically conductive metal is close to the coil, eddy currents will be induced in the metal, and this produces a magnetic field of its own." No, the wands were more like the spongy proboscises of houseflies, trailing a line of black blood instead of lapping it up. Google: labella.

The workers chatted about an overly affectionate cat that had disrupted their workday, the prospect of giving it a black stripe of sealant, an episode about "that horny skunk" remembered from childhood. For half an hour they discussed where they'd eat lunch. One of them was in favor of Whole Foods, the other Bud's. After they'd moved on, I stepped outside to examine their work. The newly laid sealant was a blacker black than the old sealant but glistened gold in the sun, veining the dull asphalt with light.

In places, the sealant pooled in shallow potholes like minia-
ture versions of the tar pits that trapped megafauna and preserved
their bones. Wikipedia: "Most tar pits are not deep enough to
actually drown an animal. The cause of death is usually starva-
tion, exhaustion from trying to escape, or exposure to the sun's
heat." Wikipedia: "Over one million fossils have been found in tar
pits around the globe." Wikipedia: "'The La Brea Tar Pits' liter-
ally means the the tar tar pits." I was bothered by places where
the workers had not dispensed enough sealant to fully pool the
concavity. It seemed as though they'd missed an opportunity to
clear a wound of dirt.

No, I realized, not *clear* the dirt. I wanted infection. Containment
of today's irritants, a burying again of the meager portion of planet

that sees light and feels the wind. Perfect infection. It seemed unfortunate to me that tire tracks already dirtied the tar in places, an irrevocable and inevitable tarnishing given the tar's consistency. Wiktionary: "tar" and "tarnish" do not share an etymology. Even if they did, tar can be tarnished—and the more dust that sticks to it, the more it's mashed by tires, the more that it's weathered by sun and snow, the less you notice it. Unlike the usual tarnishing that stands out as a defect—a stain on a shirt or a death in the family—tar is tarnished into invisibility.

HOT CRACK SEAL diamond-shaped signs warned drivers, and I had the urge to test the substance. I found it quite cool and pliable. My fingerprint held its shape for longer than I cared to watch.

As there were many more cracks in the asphalt than the workers could possibly have filigreed, I wondered if they have a system for determining that this defect is fine for now while this other needs attention.

Rich, do you?

What one of the workers argued is true: at Whole Foods you can accidentally spend like fifteen dollars on a salad.

March 24th

Calvary was brought up as an option when Bri's death forced me and Gail into conversation. She suggested it might be difficult for me to live in such close proximity to Bri's resting place. I almost laughed, but that would only have provided Gail with further proof for any number of future diagnoses.

I had to Google my neighborhood to confirm the name of the cemetery I walk by every day. There's no trusting brains anymore. Turns out it contains a grave famous enough for Google Maps to pushpin. Lilly E. Gray's tombstone reads *Victim of the Beast 666*.

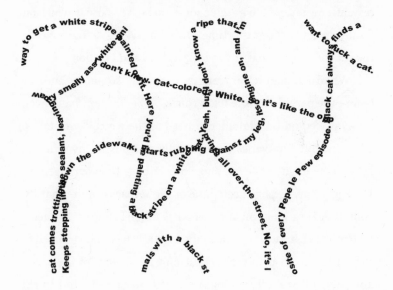

March 26th

It's one month since Bri's death, and I could tell at our session this morning that one month is Rich's milestone for tiptoeing the concept of forgiveness into the conversation. A difficult homily to a man who walks the streets for hours every night looking for blood. I didn't respond well at the session, but now I have a moment to consider what makes forgiveness so fraught in this situation. I've tried to imagine him (I've imagined him a him) with generosity, someone beaten down by society, someone sick and poor who met the wrong prophets at the wrong time. I imagine him ignorant of his actions' consequences—or, knowing, bereft. A story of the Aves and the Ave-Nots. I imagine him as Arthur, a tenant I evicted from my Liberty Park rental a few years ago. I've had to evict tenants before when they've fallen behind, promised they would pay me back if I could just give them more time—but Arthur was the only one who I believed and evicted anyway. It's a stupid, impossible fantasy, just my attempt to imagine some kind of scenario in which our family deserves this misfortune. Once I imagined Arthur's face on the shadows I screened, it was locked there and I couldn't shake it.

When I imagine forgiveness, I imagine someone kneeling before the party he or she has wronged, a benevolent hand eventually placed on the shoulder or head of the wrongdoer. Rays of sunlight. But forgiveness is especially noxious in my situation because he might not even know he's wronged me, wronged Bri. He might have experienced none of the setbacks in life that I've conjured. Forgiving someone who has not asked for it, someone who might right now be continuing to enact the potential need for forgiveness from any number of strangers . . . Perhaps the person and the guilt we're forgiving is always a projection, but in this case what I'd be forgiving is not another human, but a faltering within myself.

And, currently: no.

March 28th
I haven't sat down at the computer in my home office for a while, but today I was feeling particularly anxious about Kenneth's ability

to deal with my work responsibilities in addition to his own. Saved onto my desktop, I remembered and opened, is the fake email that got me into so much trouble, the leaking of which—coinciding with Bri's death—went viral and brought about my mandatory leave.

-----Original Message-----
From: Volmer, Donald R.
Sent: Monday, February 23, 2015 12:04 AM
To: Salt Lake City Residents
Subject: No more water : (

Dear Fellow Residents of Salt Lake City and the Wasatch Front,

Hello. My name is Don Volmer, senior analyst at the Utah Geological Survey. It's my sad task to inform you today that there is no more water left. It did not snow this year on our ski resorts, which means that there is no snowpack to refill the principal basin-fill aquifer. The deep aquifer is sucked dry, and, with no water to support its weight, the upper layer of rock has collapsed. There might cur-rently be water coming out of your faucets, but please consider yourselves warned that this will soon cease to be the case. There is no more water. It's all gone. We live in the second-driest state in the nation and the average inhabitant uses 241 gallons of water per day. I suggest relocating to Michigan, where we can continue to squander this particular resource for centuries to come.

Regards,
Don Volmer
Utah Geological Survey, Senior Analyst

Free speech has its limitations. The most frequently cited example is yelling drought in a desert. Shortage during a shortage. Double sacrifice, career and daughter of Senior Analyst, to mountain gods appeased. It's barely stopped raining since the funeral.

March 30th

With nothing else to do, I drove two hours today and visited the *Spiral Jetty* for the first time in my life. Surrogate brain: "The sculpture becomes submerged whenever the level of the Great Salt Lake rises above an elevation of 4,195 feet (1,279 m). At the time of *Spiral Jetty*'s construction, the water level of the lake was unusually low due to drought. Within a few years, the water level returned to normal, submerging the jetty for the next three decades. In 2002, the area experienced another drought, lowering the water level in the lake and revealing the jetty for a second time. The jetty remained completely exposed for almost a year. During the spring of 2005, the lake level rose again due to a near-record-setting snowpack in the surrounding mountains, partially submerging the sculpture.

In spring 2010, lake levels receded and the sculpture was again walkable and visible. Current condition fluctuate."

That's either from Wikipedia or the ether, but I searched "current condition fluctuate" to check the typo moments after copying, pasting, navigating back—and the phrase had vanished from the entry in its entirety, edited away by some stranger somewhere. Current condition do not fluctuate, apparently. It's our confident knowledge that's suffering constant erosion.

I walked the length of the jetty to the center, my sneakers collaborating with the land art's entropy. Back to my car, however, was a straight line.

A couple hundred yards south of the jetty are the lithic remains of an oilrig from the 1950s.

Oil seeps from the lakebed where the petrified temple of old dock posts jut skyward. The scabby crust has the texture of tree bark, until you stab through it.

The oil, you can play with it.

And, like tree bark, it eats irritants at glacial pace.

April 1st

Today I started learning a piano piece just because its name is cool, Debussy's prelude *La cathédrale engloutie* (*The Sunken Cathedral*). Now I remember why I had to give up relearning the piano some years ago. I always told myself, starting back in, that my life would be enhanced if I could just play, say, that one Chopin mazurka I love so much. But then my usual human affinity for the number three would make me want to learn two more pieces, perhaps become a Chopin expert of sorts. No, I would learn one piece— or three pieces—from all the major movements in old music: baroque, classical, romantic, modern. Pretty soon, one hour of practice a day would become two, three, and I'd again recall that I seem unable to just dabble in piano.

Wikipedia: "This piece is based on an ancient Breton myth in which a cathedral, submerged underwater off the coast of the Island of Ys, rises up from the sea on clear mornings when the water is transparent. Sounds can be heard of priests chanting, bells chiming, and the organ playing, from across the sea."

I'm also remembering that the more you try to channel passion or sadness or joy from your real life into your performance, the more you tend to botch it. Your mind must operate like the eyes of a driver on a highway whose exit is coming up pretty soon. Don't look at the pavement right in front of the car, the actual notes you're playing right now. No, roam the middle distance.

April 2nd

At night I've made it a habit of walking on the street rather than on the sidewalk, mainly because so many of my neighbors have motion sensor lamps with the wattage of a prison guard tower spotlight—and/or hyperactive dogs who don't know they live in the Avenues. These streets are quiet at the hours I walk, but I'm always alert for cars, especially since I've been dressing in darker and darker clothes in anticipation of meeting Arthur. Tonight—I guess it's last night technically—I heard the sound of a car approaching me from behind. I stepped aside, but something was different than usual. The car didn't have its headlights on. Then it did—its red and blue strobes as well.

The cop got out of the car and began to approach me. Backlit, her features were indiscernible to me even as I was blasted with light for her full scrutiny.

"Sir, may I speak with you for a moment?"

"Is there a problem, officer?" I delivered my line.

"Can I ask if you have any weapons on you?"

I told her that I had a crowbar, if that counted as a weapon, and I set it down on the pavement. Yes, that is my only weapon. This bag contains a camera. I handed her my camera bag. She unzipped it and gave it a fleeting inspection.

"What are you doing out here tonight?"

"I'm just out for a walk."

"Why are you carrying a camera and a crowbar?"

I didn't reply.

She continued, "There have been reports of a suspicious man walking around the neighborhood, filming. And we've had a problem with theft of manhole covers in Salt Lake City recently, including in this neighborhood. Would you know anything about this?"

I was in possession of such exact answers to her questions that I struggled to articulate them. She seemed to interpret my silence as resistance.

"Do you live in this neighborhood?"

"Yes," I said, "I live on 1st Avenue. The man with the camera is probably me, but I haven't been shooting video, just taking stills for this project I'm working on."

"Project?"

"The theft of manhole covers is why I'm out here. Like the neighborhood watch."

"It seems that the neighborhood watch is worried about the neighborhood watch."

The sign was disconcerting to me as a kid. I thought the leering black figure *was* the neighborhood watch, rather than a caricature of the type of man the watch wanted to scare off. (We've all imagined him a him.) I never liked the straight line from the tip of his hat to the small of his back. I never liked how the forbidding red bar obscures any tapering of his midsection, as if his gumshoe hat is the peak of a crooked mountain. His hat spins like a top when he's excited—I'm not sure why, but it does. I still can't figure out the slice in the side of his head. If it's a lecherous grin, then he has an eye at his ear region or a mouth on his cheek. Is that the collar of his trench coat or the jut of a bottom jaw? I guess maybe he's talking out of the side of his mouth? *Psssst* . . .

"Why do you have a crowbar with you?"

"Why hasn't the city installed locking manhole covers?"

"I want you to come down to the station with me just so we can clear a few things up. Are the photographs you've taken still on this camera?"

I didn't want to get taken down to the station or sit in the back of her car while she sorted things out.

So I told her.

April 3rd

TAKE SHORTCUT

X

Venn overlap of tragedy and comedy. Our cities are pocked with holes—but as we drive through the rainy night, we trust that the covers will be in place. Rather, we don't even think about it. Maybe tomorrow or next week, but no hole will open in my life today or today or today.

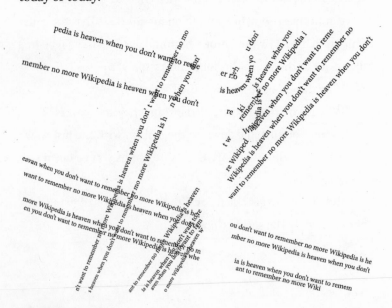

April 5th

Rich asked me at my session this morning if I think I'm making any progress. I wanted to tell him that the question is stupid. What is progress, grieving less or grieving more?

But maybe I am. Just one month ago I was asking road sealant to form the letters of the Latin alphabet. While I continue to be suspicious that all things visible and invisible are a form of writing, I'm beginning to understand that they speak to us each in their own distinct languages, and that any attempt at augury—inevitably biased and imperfect—requires translation. Maybe this is what separates artists from the rest of us.

Desperate our clinging to this crust. Fragile our traction. How utterly dictated by coincidence is all life on this planet, even more so the circumstances that impossibly collided to make me this creature here and now rather than someone else some other time, some worm, or continued nothingness—all the possibilities of existence and nonexistence in the infinite combinatory of life. So maybe I can stop holding court against one tragic coincidence, zoom out and count the heap of flukes that endow me with the love and sorrow and language to name them. Maybe I can start a new grief journal that grieves my lost daughter instead of myself.

Victim of the beast?

No, two dots in time and space wretchedly intersected. That is all.

In my dream I must have gotten a job as a city utilities worker, because I'd taken the liberty of bringing home some equipment. The tar tank had a pull cord and started like an outboard engine. My first line of black tar was reserved for her laptop. I coated the keys, the screen, the speakers, the mouse, the hinge where it closes. I sealed the line between her mattress and headboard, headboard and wall, all along her pillow. You'd need a knife to open her closet and chest of drawers after I'd finished with them. Her alarm clock would be unable to awaken a soul.

I covered the mirror in Bri's bedroom—the image of the Creator shrinks with the death of its creatures—then all the mirrors in the house. The task of containment felt incomplete, and I applied a line of sealant all around her doorframe, my dream-physics causing it to stay put and not drizzle down the door. I tarred all the framed family photographs on the walls, and when I stepped back, saw that my work spelled out *the the tar tar pits*. Following some alterations, my upright piano featured thirty-six black keys and fifty-two black keys. My cell phone and camera were encased where they sat. Let the windows be shut upon me.

Still dissatisfied that some therapist or third dot might disturb our hard-fought solitude, I applied a hot mouth seal and blindfold—so that, should I ever make it back, I would never be able to betray the route to friends or enemies.

Thank You

To my writing teachers, especially Lance Olsen, Melanie Rae Thon, Michael Mejia, Stephen Graham Jones, Craig Dworkin, and Christine Hume.

To Linda Bruckheimer, for sponsoring the Series in Kentucky Literature.

To all the people at Sarabande Books, especially Sarah Gorham and Kristen Miller.

To all of the editors and readers who allowed these stories to crash on the couches of their classy publications before they pulled themselves together, often under new names, and found a place of their own: "Opportunity Is Missed by Most People" in *Hobart*, "Earshot—Grope—Cessation" in *Passages North*, "Unearth" in *North Dakota Quarterly*, "Is it in you?" in Robert Lopez's *No News Today*, "Cover the Earth" in *New Delta Review*, "Game in the Sand" in *Heavy Feather Review*, "Lucky Girl" in *TLR: The Literary Review*, "The Unquestionable Sincerity of Fire Alarms" in *Juked*, "Make/ Shift" in *Salt Hill*, "Nepenthe" in *Booth*, and "Enough Sealant to Pool the Concavity" in the *Florida Review*. Special thanks to Robert Stapleton, Lito Velázquez, and the good folks at Write616.

To Caitlin Horrocks, Laura Kasischke, Matt Bell, and Tessa Fontaine, for your inspiring stories and your generous endorsements.

To all the friends I found at the University of Utah, especially Susannah Nevison, David Butcher, Sara Eliza Johnson, Jason Daniels, Michelle Donahue, and JP Grasser.

To my family, for supporting me even when the stories were weird.

Born in Louisville, Kentucky, **JOE SACKSTEDER** is a PhD candidate in creative writing at the University of Utah, where he serves as managing editor of *Quarterly West*. His album *Fugitive Traces* is available from Punctum Books, and his first novel, *Driftless Quintet*, is forthcoming from Schaffner Press. His writing has appeared in *Salt Hill*, *Ninth Letter*, *Denver Quarterly*, *The Rumpus*, and elsewhere.

SARABANDE BOOKS is a nonprofit literary press located in Louisville, KY. Founded in 1994 to champion poetry, short fiction, and essay, we are committed to creating lasting editions that honor exceptional writing. For more information, please visit sarabandebooks.org.